## "Rachel, what did the kidnapper say?"

In a whisper, Rachel replied, "'You can save your daughter if you mess up this kidnapping case. If you come after me, I will kill her.'"

"I recommend you back away from the investigation," Dallas said quietly.

Her head jerked up. "I can't. At least there's a better chance of finding her if I help." Her eyes glistened. "Do you have any idea what I'm going through? My daughter is in danger because of me."

Dallas grasped her shoulders. "No. She's in danger because there are evil people in this world."

"She's probably crying right now. She won't understand what's happening to her." One wet track after another coursed down Rachel's face.

Dallas wrapped his arms around her and brought her against him, sheltering her the best he could. He wasn't even sure if he should be on the case anymore because he had a score to settle with the people responsible. But Rachel needed his help to find Katie.

There was no way he would walk away...

**Margaret Daley**, an award-winning author of ninety books (five million sold worldwide), has been married for over forty years and is a firm believer in romance and love. When she isn't traveling, she's writing love stories, often with a suspense thread, and corralling her three cats, who think they rule her household. To find out more about Margaret, visit her website at margaretdaley.com.

Visit the Author Profile page at Harlequin.com for more titles.

# TEXAS BABY PURSUIT

## MARGARET DALEY

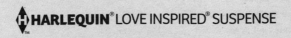

HARLEQUIN® LOVE INSPIRED® SUSPENSE

Recycling programs
for this product may
not exist in your area.

LOVE INSPIRED BOOKS

ISBN-13: 978-1-335-49053-7

Texas Baby Pursuit

Copyright © 2018 by Margaret Daley

www.Harlequin.com

Printed in U.S.A.

The Lord is my light and my salvation; whom shall I fear?
the Lord is the strength of my life;
of whom shall I be afraid?
—*Psalms* 27:1

To my two granddaughters, Abbey and Aubrey

# ONE

Texas Ranger Dallas Sanders parked in the back of the sheriff's station in Cimarron Trail, his home for the past few years. Although he worked out of the Texas Rangers' office in San Antonio, he loved returning to the smaller town northwest of the city at the end of a long day at work. Now that he'd wrapped up an intense case involving a turf war between two rival gangs that had lasted six months, it was time he introduced himself to the new sheriff, and then all he wanted to do was go to his ranch and spend quality time with his daughter, Michelle.

When he slid from his SUV and started for the building, his cell phone's ringtone played "The Yellow Rose of Texas." He smiled when he saw who was calling him. "Hi, princess. I should be home in half an hour."

"Dad, I'm not at the ranch. I'm babysitting for Aunt Lenora. Grandma drove me here, and Aunt Lenora will bring me home in a couple of hours."

His thirteen-year-old daughter was the reason he'd bought a small ranch right outside of Cimarron Trail rather than living in San Antonio. Yes, it added an hour to his commute to and from work, but it was worth it. Some of his relatives lived nearby, and after his wife had walked out on their marriage, his daughter needed family around her for support. "How about dinner?" he asked as he opened the rear door into the sheriff's station.

"I'll let you know. Aunt Lenora has a committee meeting that might run over. If I get hungry, she has stuff to eat here. The reason I'm calling is that the store where I want to buy my electronic keyboard is open until nine, and I'll have enough money after Aunt Lenora pays me. Can you take me later when I come home?"

He glanced at his watch. Three o'clock. All he had thought about on his drive home was relaxing and spending some quality time with Michelle now that he didn't have to put in fourteen-hour days.

"Dad, please."

He released a long breath. "Sure, if we have time. If not, we can go tomorrow. I'm taking a few days off."

"I think I called the wrong number. Are you sure you're Dallas Sanders?"

He laughed. "I know, princess. I've been working way too much, but I promise I'll make it up to you."

"I'm holding you to it. Gotta go. Brady's crying."

When he disconnected the call, he slid his phone back into his pocket. He smiled as he scanned the large room where most of the deputies worked. Michelle was his life. When Patricia left him a few years ago for another man, he'd spiraled into a depression that he'd had to fight his way out for the sake of his daughter. Without Michelle, he might have wallowed in his misery for years.

Dallas approached Deputy Carson, a member of his church. "Mark, is the new sheriff here?"

The young man gestured toward a closed door off the main room. "I know you don't work this county, but I was expecting you last week."

"I was working a big case that rapidly blew up. The good thing is we have the main perpetrators safely in jail now. My life will get back to normal."

Mark chuckled. "But for how long?"

"Please don't say that. I want only positive thoughts." Dallas strolled to the closed door and knocked.

"Come in," a female voice said.

He entered the office and found a woman dressed in a brown uniform with her head bent over a paper she was writing on. His gaze latched onto her shoulder-length auburn hair, which fell forward, framing her face as she looked up at him. Crystal-clear green eyes locked on his face for a few seconds before she noticed the Texas Ranger star pinned to his white shirt over his heart.

She rose, came around her desk and extended her hand. "I'm Sheriff Rachel Young. Since you aren't the Texas Ranger who covers my county—because he's on vacation—I'm assuming you're here on one of your cases. How can I help you?"

He shook her hand. "I'm Dallas Sanders, and no, I'm not here on a case. I live right outside of Cimarron Trail and wanted to welcome you to the area as well as let you know if you ever need extra help, I live at the Five Star Ranch. I understand you were a sergeant for the Austin Police Department before becoming sheriff."

Her smile lit up her whole face and made him feel at

ease. "When my father retired, I jumped at the chance to fill his position and run for sheriff. I grew up in Cimarron Trail."

"I dealt with your dad a couple of times when a case I was on involved this county, too. I didn't think he would retire for years."

"He finally decided to become a rancher. It was a childhood dream besides being a police officer. His place is northeast of Cimarron Trail. The Safe Haven Ranch, which is really a refuge for abandoned animals, is three hundred acres, small by Texas standards." She gestured toward a chair in front of her desk. "If you have time, take a seat. I'd like your view of what's happening in the area. I want to be proactive rather than reactive. My first ten days have been quiet. Too quiet. I feel like I'm waiting for the other shoe to drop."

Dallas sat while the sheriff took another chair nearby. "I assume your father filled you in."

"About the county, yes. But what I mean by the area is the other counties nearby, including Bexar County."

"I just wrapped up a case involving a turf war between two gangs. At least for the moment it's quiet between them, although I'm not naive enough to think that will last. There has also been smuggling activities up and down I-35."

His cell phone sounded, and he slipped it from his pocket to see who was calling. Michelle. Again? Maybe her plans watching Brady had changed. She usually texted him while he was working, but a call twice in fifteen minutes was most unusual. "I need to answer this."

He tapped the on button. "Michelle—"

"Help! They're taking Brady!"

Her frantic words, followed by a scream, urged Dallas to his feet. "Michelle, what's going on?"

Then it sounded like she dropped the phone, sending chills down his spine. "No! Don't," she cried out.

"Michelle!" Everything went silent.

He rushed out into the main room, aware the sheriff had followed him. He glanced back. "Something's happened at my sister's house. Can you follow me?"

With her keys in her hand, the sheriff nodded and said to a deputy, "Follow, too."

As Dallas hurried toward his SUV, he kept repeating his daughter's name into his cell phone, but there was only silence. The phone was dead. His heart pounded against his ribcage as he started his car. His sister's house wasn't far from the sheriff's station, but every scenario involving kids that he'd encountered as a law enforcement officer raced through his thoughts. He recalled the semi truck full of human beings smuggled into the United States—children included—discovered just this month in a parking lot during the heat of summer in a suburb of San Antonio.

After he slammed to a stop in his sister's driveway, he ran toward the front door, trying not to think about the smuggling rings bringing people in and out of this country. He couldn't rid his mind of it. Fear spurred him to go faster.

When he spied the front door wide open he drew his gun, and his professional facade fell into place. Whatever had gone down, the perpetrator could still be inside—with his daughter.

Sheriff Young and her deputy entered the house right behind him. Dallas motioned for them to go right while he went left toward the bedrooms. His heartbeat drowned out other sounds as he moved down the hall, checking the rooms. When he stepped into Brady's, its emptiness mocked him. *Brady is gone. Where is Michelle?*

As Rachel moved into the kitchen, the first thing she noticed was that the back door—just like the front door—was wide open. She gestured for her deputy to circle the room while she headed to the exit, leading to a screened-in porch.

Lying on a blanket on the wood floor was a young teenage girl, her arm stretched out toward a smashed cell phone, blood pooling onto the coverlet. "Call 911," Rachel yelled to her deputy as she rushed to the child and knelt next to her.

The girl's eyes fluttered, opened for a few seconds, then closed.

"Michelle. I'm here to help. Your dad is, too." Rachel felt the teenager's pulse on the side of her neck. Her fast heart rate might indicate a concussion. She examined the injury on the side of the girl's head, blood still flowing from it, but she couldn't tell how deep the wound was. "Michelle."

The young teen moaned and lifted her eyelids as she tried to sit up.

Rachel gently restrained her. "Don't get up yet." She spied a white hand towel on the blanket and snatched it up, then pressed it against the girl's wound to try and stop the bleeding.

The child's brown eyes grew wide as she stared over Rachel's shoulder. "Dad."

Rachel had been so absorbed in the teenager she hadn't heard Dallas coming out onto the porch. She looked over her shoulder at Texas Ranger Dallas Sanders, over six feet tall. His stiff posture and clenched jaw warred with the smile flirting at the edges of his mouth as he looked at his daughter.

A half grin won out. "I'm here, honey. You'll be okay. I promise."

Rachel was amazed at the calmness in his voice. Now she understood why her father had mentioned Dallas when discussing potential allies for her in the area. He kept his composure in a situation that would throw most into a panic.

Dallas squatted on the other side of Michelle and took over putting pressure on the injury to stem the blood flow. "What happened?" he asked in a soft, soothing voice.

"Brady." Michelle turned her head to the side—the movement causing her to wince and displace the cloth on her wound. "They…took him, Daddy." She waved her hand toward an area with scattered toys on the blanket. Tears ran down her face.

Again the teen tried to rise, but this time Dallas clasped one of her shoulders. "Don't move until you're checked out." He re-covered the injury with the cloth. Worry engraved deeper lines on his face.

"Your dad's right," Rachel said. "An ambulance is on its way. You're in good hands."

"But Brady…" Michelle's eyelids half closed "…is gone…" Tears drenched her cheeks, her eyes dulling.

Rachel glanced at Dallas. Their gazes locking for a few seconds gave her a brief glimpse into the suppressed fear in his eyes, so dark they were almost black. "Michelle, I'm Sheriff Young. I'm here to look for Brady. You don't need to worry. I'll take care of him."

While Dallas hovered over his daughter, trying to re-assure her everything was being taken care of, Rachel rose and covered the distance to Deputy Jones, who was one of her investigative officers. "Call for backup. A baby was taken. We need help looking for Brady." She started for the screen door that led to the yard. "I'll be out here canvassing the yard. Let me know when more help arrives."

"Yes, ma'am," her deputy said with a nod.

Rachel started for the exit, glancing back at Dallas and his daughter.

"I'll be right back, princess."

Michelle clutched her father's arm. "Don't leave me, Daddy."

"I'm not. I need to talk to the sheriff for a moment."

The teen slipped her hand away and held the cloth over her injury, her arm shaking. Dallas rose and quickly bridged the short distance between himself and Rachel. "I'll get what information I can from Michelle and contact my sister and mother."

"I'll need a description of Brady and what he was wearing, and if possible, a recent picture. It'll help with the Amber Alert. How old is he?"

"He's eight months old and crawling. Not walking yet. He has dark hair and blue eyes."

Rachel nodded, then turned toward the door as the EMTs came onto the porch. The screen door was slightly open. The kidnapper came in this way or left out the back. She descended the steps but paused a moment and again looked at Dallas, standing back from his daughter, running his fingers through his short brown hair. A tic twitched in his jaw while one of the paramedics stooped to check Michelle.

Rachel's throat thickened. She had a daughter who would turn one in a month. All she wanted to do was drive out to her parents' house, pick up Katie and hug her. Never let her go. The only good thing that had come out of her marriage was Katie.

This case would be hard for her. She'd only been sheriff for a couple of weeks and had dealt with minor crimes so far. The honeymoon was over.

She scanned the area—open with few fences except one along the back where a dirt road ran behind the houses on the street. The kidnapper could have parked on that road by the southern border of the Fowlers' ranch and easily climbed the rear fence. But then, if that were case, why was the front door open?

As she walked toward the rear of the property, using the most direct path, her gaze swept the ground around her. About ten feet away, she spotted a binky on the grass. She took out her phone and snapped a picture. After putting on a pair of gloves, she leaned over, picked up the blue pacifier and put it into an evidence bag. From the looks of it, it hadn't been outside long. Possibly dropped by Brady, which meant the kidnappers had left by the back door and headed for the road behind the house. She'd need to know from Michelle how the kidnappers got into the house, since both entrances were wide open.

Most likely the perpetrators entered through the front door, because it had been wide open when Michelle and Dallas arrived. Maybe they fled out the nearest exit. And ran around to the front to leave? She hoped a neighbor had seen something—the kidnappers or the getaway car with a license plate number.

It was even possible they'd come into the place

through the back screen door and gone out the front because their car was on the street. But wouldn't Michelle have seen them approaching from the rear? Only the top half of the porch was screened. Rachel shook her head and looked back at the house.

Her stomach tightened into a hard ball, and she held up the evidence bag with the binky in it. Or they'd come in the front and gone out the back, their car parked on the dirt road behind the property. She had to check everything out. Timing was important in cases like kidnapping.

She climbed the fence rails and paused above the ground and road, staring at several sets of different tire tracks. She knew they were freshly made because the day before it had rained hard. She would have casts made of all of them. Maybe one would give them a lead. She inspected the barren earth that had only a few weeds sticking up. Two pairs of boot prints crisscrossed the tire tracks. Michelle had said "they." Were there two intruders or more, having something to do with one of the back ways into the Fowlers' ranch?

She would have this area blocked off and processed, but she would also need to pay Houston Fowler a visit to find out which of his employees had used this road in the past twenty-four hours. Even if no one had, maybe one of them saw something.

As she hopped down and started back toward the house, her cell phone rang. She glanced at the caller ID and punched the on button. "Is everything all right, Dad?"

"I've got a call there's been a kidnapping."

"An eight-month-old baby."

"Whose?"

"Lenora and Paul Howard's. How's Katie?"

"She's fine. Your mother is feeding her. Don't worry. I won't let anything happen to my granddaughter."

Her dad knew her well. Rachel reached the porch. "I need to go."

"I don't want to butt in, but I'll help in any way you need."

"Thanks, Dad. Right now, just keep Katie safe." Rachel disconnected the call and opened the screen door to the porch, then entered.

Deputy Jones finished taking photos of the area. "Texas Ranger Sanders went with his daughter to the regional hospital."

Thinking of the nasty bleeding gash on the side of Michelle's head, Rachel asked, "Was she still responsive when she left?"

"Yes. He called his sister and brother-in-law. They should be here soon. Also, the word's getting out and already a couple of reporters have arrived."

"But not on the property?"

"No. Standing in the street along with some of the neighbors."

"I'll go around front and meet the parents. Send a deputy out to make castings of the tire tracks along the dirt road behind here as well as the two sets of boot prints."

Instead of going through the house, Rachel headed around the side of the building and came upon a large, muscular man wearing a hoodie standing behind a group of tall bushes, peeking in a window. When he spied her, he whirled around, plunged through the thick vegetation and raced across the Howards' neighbor's back lawn.

Rachel took out after him. Her heart pounded as quickly as her feet against the ground. The suspicious man disappeared around the corner of a home two away from the Howards'. As she chased him, she pressed her mic and said, "I'm in pursuit of a guy at the Howards'. I'm two houses away heading west. I need backup."

Who was this guy? Why was he there? What was he looking for?

Rachel chased the man around the side of the neighbor's place, colliding into the solid wall of his body, his head down, hood masking his face. She stumbled back, fighting to stay on her feet. As she regained her footing, she raised her head just as a fist plowed into her jaw, then her eye. The world swirled, and she collapsed.

# TWO

Rachel slammed against the ground, pain radiating through her face where she'd been hit. The air rushed from her lungs. Dragging in shallow breaths, she hurriedly tried to stand, but her ears rang and dizziness swirled her vision, one eye watering where her assailant had struck her. Punching the button on her mic, she said, "I need help," a few seconds before Deputy Jones rounded the corner of the house and rushed to her.

"Are you okay?" The deputy made a quick scan of the area then squatted next to her.

Rachel gently felt the left side of her jaw and winced. "The suspect I was chasing had a strong right hook."

"Which way did he go?" Jones stood.

"He's long gone by now." Again, she attempted to stand, this time using Deputy Jones's offered hand, and managed to remain upright although it felt like a bell was continuously clanging in her head. She filled him in on why she was chasing the guy who had assaulted her. "I need to check the area under that window. I found boot prints on the dirt road behind the Howards' house. This guy had boots on." Had she encountered one of the kidnappers? He'd taken her by surprise. She hadn't expected anyone looking in a window at the crime scene not long after the crime had happened and with the police on-site. When she increased her pace, her world spun. She stumbled, would have gone down if her deputy hadn't grabbed her.

"Ma'am, I'm taking you to the hospital. You need to be checked out. I'll let Deputy Carson know about the intruder and where he was. He'll look into it."

She started to protest. She had an investigation to oversee. A crime to solve—quickly. But her stomach roiled, and she leaned against Deputy Jones, closing her eyes. "Okay." She hadn't wanted to show any weakness in the first month of being the sheriff. She'd overheard a couple of her deputies recently saying that the only reason she'd won the election was because her father had been sheriff. She was determined to prove she was a better person for the job than the guy who'd run against her, Marvin Compton.

Hours later, Dallas paced the Cimarron Trail Regional Hospital room while his daughter finally went to sleep—although Michelle wouldn't be getting much rest overnight here. He wanted to be out there hunting down the people who had done this to Michelle. Clenching his fists, he tried to work the rage and tension from himself. He needed to be focused and was determined to find out who took his nephew and left his daughter to possibly bleed out.

The door opened slowly. It was too soon for the nurse to be checking on Michelle again. While he swung around to see who it was, every muscle in his body constricted, preparing to protect her.

When Sheriff Rachel Young poked her head into the room relief drove the tightness from his stance. His shoulders slumped as he leaned against the bed, taking in the reddening skin around her eye and swelling on the left side of her jaw. "What happened?"

"I ran into a fist."

"One of the kidnappers?"

"Don't know. He got away, but the doc who checked me out earlier said I'll look like a chipmunk trying to store food for the winter, not to mention my shiner." She glanced at Michelle, sleeping, her head bandaged. "You called Deputy Jones and told him what your daughter said about the abduction. I want to make sure we have the correct information before I move forward with the investigation. Is this a good time to talk?"

He slanted a look at Michelle. "This is fine." He gestured toward the loveseat and chair in the hospital room.

When Rachel took a seat in the chair, he sat on the couch catty-corner from her. "It's not much. She'll probably remember more later. She said there were two people—a woman and a man."

"What did they look like?"

"She couldn't tell me much. All she could say was the woman had large dark sunglasses and big blond hair. The man had a mask on."

"What kind?"

"A black ski mask."

"Did she see what color his eyes were? How tall he was?"

Dallas remembered Michelle crying as she talked about the kidnappers. "All she said about him was that he was taller than her and the woman with him."

"How did they get into the house?"

"She blames herself. She opened the front door to the woman. Then the woman barged into the house and Michelle ran toward where she'd left Brady sleeping on the blanket. The first time she saw the guy was on the screened-in porch. He'd kicked the door in and was standing over my nephew. After that, she doesn't remember much."

"Why did she open the door to the woman?"

Dallas let out a long breath. "Normally she wouldn't open the door, but my sister told her that a lady was bringing over a file she needed for the committee Lenora is on. Michelle thought she was that woman. Have you talked to my sister yet?"

"Briefly, right before I came back to the hospital to talk to you and Michelle. Lenora kept asking for you. Your brother-in-law called her doctor, who came over and gave her a sedative. She'd barely been able to answer even simple questions, like when she left the house. I'd like you to be there when I talk to her the next time. Paul's supposed to let me know when she wakes up."

"When did Paul arrive home?"

"Fifteen minutes after your sister. She kept asking where you and your mother were."

"I've been trying to get hold of Mom. She has a tendency of silencing her cell phone. She only has one for times she wants to get hold of someone or for emergencies. I left her a voice message and texted her. Hopefully she'll use the phone and notice them."

"Where is she?"

"This is her day to run errands so she could be many places. Once a month she goes to San Antonio.

I don't know if that's today or not. Has the Amber Alert gone out?"

"Yes. Paul gave me a current photo of Brady, and Lenora told me what he was wearing."

Exhausted from the past months of working a tough case, Dallas glanced at Michelle. He had to pull himself together. He couldn't rest until he found the kidnappers. What if they came back after Michelle? Her head injury was serious, and she'd lost quite a lot of blood. They'd left her to die, and she could have if he and Rachel hadn't gotten there in time. When the kidnappers discovered she hadn't, they might come after her again. "Michelle saw the woman and might be able to pick her out in a lineup."

"Wearing sunglasses and possibly a wig?"

"Yeah. Michelle loves to draw and is quite good at it. She might be able to sketch a picture of her. She remembers things like that. She told me once she looked at the world through an artist's eyes."

Rachel checked her watch. "Deputy Jones dropped me off and took the evidence in to the station. We need to process what little we have as quickly as possible. I told him I'd be in here with you, and I'd call him to pick me up after I talked to you. I'm officially asking you to help with the case. I know you've got a personal stake in this, but if I were you, I'd be investigating— whether or not I'd been asked to assist. This way we can coordinate with each other."

"What do you know so far?"

"Paul couldn't think of a reason for anyone to take Brady. Most likely, the kidnappers had left out the rear screen door, crossed the yard and climbed the fence. After the recent rain, there were only one set of unique tire tracks and two different sets of boot prints, one much larger than the other, which supports what Michelle told you that there's a woman and a man involved. Possibly a couple who wanted a baby?"

Dallas frowned. "Coming into a house is risky, but then, maybe they knew my sister left Brady with Michelle. I have a call in to Texas Ranger headquarters. I want to know if other babies have been taken in recent months in the area, especially snatched from their homes. This could also be part of a baby smuggling ring or people brokering illegal adoptions."

Rachel massaged her temples. "I know. I've been considering that aspect, too. I called the FBI to see if they know anything about a ring operating in this part of Texas."

Dallas received a call and quickly answered it. "Mom, I'm glad you called. Have you talked with Lenora yet?"

"No, I got a call from Paul and was going to talk to him after you. What's going on?"

"Are you driving?"

"I'm at a gas station about ten miles from Cimarron Trail."

"Are you sitting down?"

"Son, you're scaring me. What happened?"

Dallas wished he didn't have to tell her over the phone. "A couple of hours ago Brady was kidnapped while Michelle was babysitting him. She was attacked and now she's in the hospital with a severe concussion. She has ten stitches on the side of her head." When his mother didn't say anything for a long moment, he asked, "Mom, are you all right?"

"No," she replied with a sob. "How could this happen? Cimarron Trail is a quiet town."

"I wish I had an answer for you, but I promise you and Lenora I'll work on this case until it's solved. No one hurts my family." The hand clutching the cell phone ached from his tight hold. "They left Michelle there bleeding and…" His words jammed in his throat.

"Are you at the regional hospital with her?"

"Yes. She's sleeping."

"I'm headed straight there. I'll sit with her. You need to find Brady. I'll call Paul and let him know what I'm doing."

Before Dallas could say anything else, his mother disconnected. He dropped his arm to his side while he stared at the bed where Michelle lay sleeping.

A hand touched him. "What's wrong?"

Rachel's soft words brought him out of his trance. He blinked then swung his attention to the sheriff. "My mother's coming here. She wants to sit with Michelle while I search for Brady, but I can't leave her unprotected. And yet my sister needs to know I won't give up until her son is found."

"Of course, you won't. She knows that." Their gazes connected. The comfort in Rachel's eyes pulled him in, and for a few seconds nothing else existed.

"I'll have one of my deputies stand guard outside the room. Michelle is the only witness we have. She'll be safe."

"The only way my daughter will be safe is when I bring in the two people who hurt her and took Brady."

"Daddy…"

The whispered word twisted his heart. Michelle had

stopped calling him daddy years ago. He rushed over to the bed. "You're supposed to be resting, princess."

"I can't—" she ran her tongue over her lips "—with Brady gone."

"Do you want water?"

"Yes," Michelle said, her eyelids slowly closing.

Dallas snatched up the pitcher and quickly filled a plastic cup that held a straw. When he swiveled his attention back to her, her eyes eased open again. He helped her to sit up, then held the cup while she slowly sipped through the straw.

After he carefully laid her back against the bed, she said, "Find him. Please…for me." Then she surrendered to sleep again.

Still holding the plastic cup, he dropped his head, torn, wishing he could be in two places at once.

Rachel was moved at the exchange between Dallas and Michelle. With her head still pounding from the punches she'd taken, she rose slowly, crossed the hospital room and stood next to him, her hand brushing against his. "I'm so sorry this happened to your daughter."

Lines creased his forehead as he looked down at her. Sadness shadowed his eyes. "Call a deputy. When my mom gets here, I'll go with you to help, at least with Lenora. I'm really worried about her. She lost two babies before Brady and was on bed rest the last month of her pregnancy with him. The doctor hasn't encouraged her to have another child."

She could only imagine the grief and pain Lenora was going through right now. "I'll make a call." She pulled out her cell phone, walking away a few feet.

Although Michelle was asleep, Rachel didn't want the teen to hear about placing a deputy outside her room.

When Rachel reached the dispatcher, she lowered her voice. "Maddy, send a deputy to the regional hospital to room 208. Have him knock on the door."

"Will do. Deputy Ellis just came in."

"Thanks. Any calls concerning the kidnapping?"

"Yeah, I'm keeping a log. Most are wondering what's going on. I told them what you said about having a press conference tomorrow morning."

"Great, Maddy. Thanks."

Rachel hit the off button and turned toward Dallas at the same time the door flew open and a petite, dark-haired woman made a beeline for the hospital bed and him.

His mother's hand covered her mouth while she shook her head. "She looks so lost in that bed." The older woman stood next to Dallas. "What's wrong with the world that someone would do this?"

"I wish I could answer that." His gaze connected with Rachel's while he held his mother against him. "I feel so much better having you here. Your nurse's training will come in handy."

His mother leaned back. "I may be retired, but I still know what I'm doing. You have nothing to worry about. I talked with Paul. Lenora was still sleeping." She glanced over her shoulder and slipped from her son's loose embrace. "I'm Dottie Sanders. You must be Bill's daughter. I voted for you."

"Thanks for the vote, Mrs. Sanders. I have Deputy Ellis coming to stand guard outside the door. If you need anything, let him know."

"I will. But we'll be perfectly fine. Just find my grandson," she pleaded.

As Rachel nodded, a light knock at the door sounded. "That's probably him. I'll be out in the hall when you're ready, Dallas."

In the corridor, Rachel filled Deputy Ellis in on what she wanted him to do. "The teen who was hurt is our only witness to the two people who stole the baby. Keep her safe."

"Yes, ma'am."

Dallas joined them in the hallway, shaking hands with Deputy Ellis. "I appreciate you guarding my daughter. My mom—Dottie Sanders—is in there with her."

"Thanks for letting me know."

Rachel made her way to the stairs with Dallas right next to her. Her head still hurt, but the ringing in her ears and the dizziness had faded. "I have a favor to ask. Deputy Jones brought me to the hospital, but I had him go back to your sister's house after taking the evidence to headquarters. I told him I'd call him when I needed a ride, and I wondered if you—"

He chuckled. "If this is your roundabout way of asking for a ride, then yes, I can give you one to my sister's. Is that where your car is?"

She nodded. "My ears were ringing after I was punched. Deputy Jones didn't think I should drive myself, and I can't argue with one of my dad's friends."

"I have a lot of respect for your father. I worked a case with him about eight months ago that extended over several counties." Dallas held the door open for Rachel.

"I was surprised he retired. He'd been sheriff for

twenty-five years, and it was his life. Now he and my mom watch my daughter. Actually, she has to fight him to get her chance to take care of Katie. He's always busy around the property, and Katie, who is nearly one, is getting a good lesson in how to run a ranch. Or, at least, Dad's trying to teach her."

"How does your husband feel about you being the sheriff?" Again Dallas opened a door for her.

"I'm a widow. My husband died over fifteen months ago." She slid into the front passenger seat.

"Oh, I'm sorry. I didn't know."

She had no words to reply, so she nodded.

As Dallas rounded the front of his SUV, memories inundated Rachel. How could she forgive Justin for having an affair that she didn't even know about until after he had died in a motorcycle race? The man she married wasn't who she'd thought he was. He'd said he wanted a child, and yet, in a text to his mistress that she discovered on his phone, he had said otherwise. And there she'd been, nearly two months pregnant with no husband. Never again. She wouldn't let herself be fooled like that again.

When Dallas climbed behind the steering wheel and started the car, a heavy silence fell between them, which was fine with Rachel because she didn't want to talk about her deceased husband. All her focus needed to be on the case.

"Tell me a little about your sister. Even though Paul assured me otherwise, could someone be after your sister or her husband—someone who would kidnap their baby to get back at them?"

"Lenora volunteers at church and through a woman's club. Paul is a CPA who works for Remington Industries in San Antonio. I don't think so."

"An accountant with possible access to financial records?"

Dallas stopped at the red light. "The work he does is routine. He's only been working for the company for two years. He says he's low on the totem pole. They've never indicated having a problem with anyone. They get along with their neighbors, but I don't know about everything they do during the day. My gut tells me it isn't that."

"You go by your gut a lot?"

"I never dismiss hunches. I understand you were a police sergeant for the Austin Police Department. Did you ever go on a hunch?"

"Sure."

"It's the same thing. The more we can read people, the better we are about figuring out a clue, motive or case. Take the fact a guy in a hoodie fled from the crime scene and punched you out. What was he doing there? Was he tied to the kidnappers or my sister and Paul?" The light turned green, and Dallas drove across the intersection.

"I caught him looking in the window."

"Yes, I know, but why was he doing that? Was he a reporter? Talk about fast on the scene and bold." Dallas shrugged.

"Why would a reporter punch me? Maybe he's a snooping neighbor checking out what was going on?"

"Why take the risk when he would find out soon enough on the news?"

Her first instinct was that the Peeping Tom was tied to the kidnappers, and that was still the best possibility. "He may have risked coming back if there was something left behind at the crime scene that could connect him to the kidnapping."

"Yes, that's what I've been thinking because he punched you. A neighbor or reporter wouldn't have gone to that extreme and risk being arrested."

"Deputy Jones handled the crime scene. As far as I know, nothing was found other than the footprints and tire tracks, and the pacifier I discovered in the backyard."

Dallas parked behind her sheriff's car in his sister's driveway. "It wouldn't hurt to look around again while we're here. Which window was the guy looking in?"

"I think the dining room. Everything happened so fast." Rachel scanned the crowd of people hanging around. There were two camera crews from different television stations in San Antonio as well as local folks she recognized.

"We need to recheck for anything out of the ordinary, especially with Lenora and Paul here now."

"I agree." Rachel stepped down from the SUV and headed toward the Howards' house. Working with Dallas seemed to come so naturally. She was glad he was here to help because this would be her first big test as the county sheriff.

One of her deputies stood on the front porch and another one should be at the back door. She'd hated taking time away from the investigation to go to the hospital, but at least she'd had a chance to see what else Michelle could remember and make sure she would recover. "Did Michelle say anything about the kidnappers having a gun?"

"No. She was drowsy. I was happy to get what I

could out of her. But I wouldn't be surprised if one or both had a gun. Did the guy that hit you have one?"

"I didn't see one, but when I was trying to stem the flow of blood from her wound, it looked like the kind of damage a handle of a revolver could have done."

His tanned complexion whitened. "Not that I'm complaining, but if he had a gun, why didn't he shoot her rather than hit her?"

"The noise. They still had to get away without anyone seeing them." Rachel entered his sister's house first and strode into the living area that connected with the dining room and kitchen, checking the placement of the windows on the side of the house where she'd seen the Peeping Tom and deciding she was right. The dining room was where the man had been looking inside.

Dallas came up behind and leaned toward her. "Which window was he peeking into?"

She pointed at the one on the left in the dining room. "There." She glanced over her shoulder, his face close to hers. A whiff of lime wafted to her. "Which doesn't surprise me. If the couple charged into your sister's home, the fastest way to nab Brady was through the living and dining room into the kitchen and out onto the back porch. From what you said earlier I got the impression that Brady wasn't with her when she went to the front door."

"Right. He was asleep on the pallet on the screened-in porch."

"The getaway car was most likely parked behind the property on the dirt road. Why didn't Michelle see them walking across the backyard?"

"I'm not sure. Possibly because she might have been

on the floor with Brady, and the screened part is only the top half. They might not have seen her, either. Or one went to the front to distract Michelle while the other snatched Brady." He looked toward the hallway to the bedrooms, spying his brother-in-law making his way toward them. "Paul, is Lenora awake and able to talk to us?"

She hadn't even heard Paul coming down the corridor. Her total attention had centered on Dallas. The pain in his gaze drew her to him. The thought of losing her baby pierced through her heart like a red-hot lance. Paul and Lenora were living a parent's worst nightmare.

"I'm getting her a glass of water. She should be able to talk after that." The defeat in Paul's voice filled the silence.

"We'll be out on the porch," Rachel said.

Paul nodded. "That's where Deputy Jones is." He walked past them toward the kitchen. "Dottie called and told me how Michelle was doing. I'm glad she'll be all right."

"Thanks." Dallas followed his brother-in-law into the kitchen, asking what his mother said concerning his daughter.

Rachel paused in the dining room and panned the area that held a table and six chairs and a display cabinet between the two windows. Thick, brown carpeting covered the floor. The only thing on the table was an artificial flower arrangement. She moved from one chair to the next, pulling it out and seeing if anything was on the seat. Nothing. Then she knelt and looked under the cabinet and table. A glint caught her attention near a chair. She crawled to it and saw a short gold chain with a heart charm on it buried in the long fibers of the rug.

She quickly put on gloves and picked up the bracelet. On the heart were the initials DN. Was it Lenora's? The letters didn't match her name. Until she found out, it would remain in the evidence bag she dropped it into. Usable latent prints might be on it. She hoped it was a clue that would lead them to Brady. Was the bracelet the reason the guy had been peeping in the dining room window? She wanted it to be a clue, but it was still possible the man might have nothing to do with the case.

Rachel quickly pushed to her feet, a few seconds of light-headedness hitting her. She had a mild concussion, nothing like Michelle's, but she needed to watch for any signs her concussion was worsening. She strolled into the kitchen as Paul was leaving.

Across the room Dallas looked at her, their eyes bound together for a few seconds. He broke visual contact first and sauntered in the direction of the door that led to the porch.

"I found something in the dining room."

He stopped and peered back at her, one brow raised.

She covered the distance between them and withdrew the small evidence bag from her pocket. "It's a bracelet with a heart charm that has DN engraved on it. Does this look familiar to you?"

He held it up and examined it closely. "No. I've never seen Lenora with it or my mother or even Michelle. She spends a lot of time here."

"Then this could be what the guy who hit me came back for."

"Possibly. We need to show it to Lenora and Paul.

It could belong to one of their friends I'm not familiar with."

"I will."

At the rear exit, Rachel stood in the doorway and slowly swept her gaze around the porch. Three walls were half screened on the top while the bottom was brick. The area had been childproofed and had a baby swing in a corner. When she focused on the coverlet on the wooden floor, her throat tightened at the sight of the blood on it and the cell phone Michelle used to call Dallas.

"I asked Deputy Jones to process for latent prints and search for any evidence but to leave the room as it is. I wanted you to see it when you weren't concentrating on getting your daughter to the hospital."

"Thanks. You're right. I wasn't paying much attention once I saw Michelle."

Deputy Jones appeared at the back door and came into the room. "You're gonna have one nice shiner there, sheriff."

"That's because the Peeping Tom clocked me with a one-two punch." She waved her hand at her jaw then her eye.

"I don't even have to look in a mirror to remind me that the guy got in two packed punches. Except for taking up the blanket and phone, are you finished in here?"

"Yes, ma'am. The area along the dirt road has been searched, but other than the tire tracks and boot prints, that's all we found. I had a couple of deputies comb the back and front yards, but they didn't find anything. Another deputy went to talk to Houston Fowler."

"Good. Let me know if Fowler has any information that will help this case. I want to show Dallas where I think they got away." Rachel swung her attention to Dallas, who stared at the blood, his jaws clenched so tightly a muscle twitched. "Do you want to go out back?"

He lifted his head, his eyes full of anger. While he battled for control, he marched to the outside door and left the porch.

"Bag the blanket and phone and take them to headquarters. Did we get good latent prints?" Rachel asked her deputy while watching Dallas scope out the yard.

"Yes. There were tons. I'm in the process of getting fingerprints from family members or friends who've been here recently to rule them out."

"Thanks. We'll be back."

Rachel joined Dallas, still seeing a struggle between anger and determination. She again felt a connection with him that surprised her. They were both single parents and had daughters, but the two girls were years apart in age. Where was Michelle's mother? It wasn't easy raising a child alone, as Rachel was finding out.

With his hands fisted at his sides, Dallas closed his eyes. He spread his fingers wide and shook them. The tense set of his face relaxed, and when he twisted toward her and looked at her, a calm, professional demeanor fell into place. "I have to work this case. I can't let my emotions take over."

"I know. If my daughter were kidnapped, no matter what, I would be out there looking for her."

"It won't be easy to remain objective, but with the Lord's help, I'll find out who kidnapped Brady."

"Good. We need all the help we can get." Rachel began walking across the yard.

"The castings were taken for the tire tracks and boot prints on the other side of the back fence?"

"Yes."

"Did you notice what kind of shoes the guy who hit you was wearing?"

Rachel stopped and closed her eyes, trying to picture the man running away from her. She remembered watching his hoodie, hoping it would slip from his head. When he turned the corner of the neighbor's house, had she caught sight of his shoes? "I think he was wearing black hiking boots. One of my deputies made a casting of the prints by the dining room window. I haven't had a chance yet to compare them."

Dallas climbed the fence, straddled the top and stretched out his arm to help her. She clasped his palm, his large hand swallowing her smaller one. His warm touch engulfed her in a wave of awareness that startled her. He hoisted her up. Their gazes met and held for a long moment. Finally she looked away, afraid that her cheeks were red.

When they both descended to the ground near the dirt road, she put a few feet between them, not sure what had just happened. She strolled to the boot prints. "The smaller set with the larger one fits the scenario that a man and woman took Brady. Her shoe size is about a six."

Dallas put his cowboy boot alongside the other set. "And he wears a twelve."

"Now all we have to do is find a couple who wear a shoe sizes of six and twelve."

"Just one of many clues I hope we'll find." Dallas made his way to the tire imprints. "They drove a small compact car." He took several steps between the tracks and knelt, using a pencil to move the grass. "This vehicle was leaking oil." He took out his cell phone and took a picture. "A lot. That might help us. Make sure your deputy got a sample of this oil in case we find a car leaking oil."

Dusk settled over the landscape as Dallas walked up the road toward the Fowlers' property, then came back and went in the other direction. When he returned, he said, "They turned around about a hundred yards that way." He pointed toward the ranch. "Let's go talk to Lenora and Paul. There isn't much else we can do here, and I need to return to the hospital and relieve Mom."

As they headed back to the house, Dallas received a call. He stopped and listened, the lines in his forehead getting deeper the longer the other person talked.

"How many babies were stolen?" Dallas turned his back on Rachel and lowered his voice.

More babies taken? When he ended the conversation, Rachel stiffened, preparing herself for the worst.

# THREE

As Dallas neared Lenora's porch, he clutched his cell phone. "That was the Texas Ranger office in San Antonio on the phone. There's been a series of baby snatchings north of Dallas."

"How many have there been?" Rachel asked as she moved into the house.

"Three babies were kidnapped by strangers, but that's not all. They checked throughout Texas, and one other area has reported the same crime pattern in the past year. There was a cluster of kidnappings in El Paso. I don't think this is just a couple looking for a baby."

"Which means we'll have two more before they move on, if they hold to the pattern."

He grasped her arm and stopped her before she entered the kitchen. "Sounds like a systematic organization kidnapping babies to sell. They only stay a few weeks in one area, then they move on. I'll be checking to see if this is happening in other states."

Rachel frowned. "We have to stop them."

"I've already asked headquarters to expand to the surrounding states. To see if there are cases like this there. In the meantime, I'll get what information I can about the other abductions. Maybe there's a pattern forming where others were taken from their homes. If not, we need to establish if there's one—or if the kidnappings are random with nothing in common between them."

"This is going to send this area into a panic, but it might help. People will be more vigilant. That might be a good thing."

"So long as they don't overreact." He paused in the kitchen. "When will you hold a press conference?"

"I'm releasing information tomorrow morning at eight. I want to see if your sister and brother-in-law would like to address the reporters. Right now, there are only a few outside, but by tomorrow that number will grow."

"Do you want me to be there?"

"Yes. I want whoever took Brady to know who's coming after them."

"They picked the wrong family to mess with." His words were quiet but lethal sounding.

Rachel was glad to have his assistance. The county sheriff election had been contentious and even ugly, especially toward the end when it appeared she would win. She became sheriff because of her father's good reputation and the many years he'd been in office, but the only way she would remain in the position was to do a good job, like he'd done. She couldn't let her dad down.

Rachel continued toward the living room with Dallas right behind her. Lenora sat on the couch, her head down, her hands clutching a blue knitted blanket that had been on a chair in the living room when she'd first walked through the house. All Rachel wanted to do was hug Lenora. The pain she was going through wove its way through Rachel. Katie was the most important person in her life.

Paul entered from the foyer, a scowl etching deep lines in his face. "I took the phone off the hook. It's been ringing for the past few hours, and I can't deal with it anymore." His voice rough with emotion, he took a place next to his wife and slipped his arm along her shoulders.

Rachel sank into the wingback chair across from Lenora while Dallas eased down next to his sister on her other side. "I'm so sorry for what happened. I promise I won't rest until we track down these kidnappers and find Brady. Have you noticed anything unusual lately—like a person you didn't know following or watching you more than once?"

Never looking up, Lenora shook her head.

"Has someone called and hung up when you picked up the phone?"

"No."

"Did the woman who was supposed to pick something up ever come?" Rachel pulled the evidence bag from her pocket.

Lenora's glistening eyes lifted to Rachel's face. "No, but she called me to let me know she wasn't while I was in the meeting. I should have told Michelle, but I didn't get a chance."

"Who is the friend?" Rachel would need to check out the woman.

"Mary Jane Martin. I've known her for years." One tear ran down Lenora's face, then another. "If I had let Michelle know she wasn't coming right away, this might not have happened. It's all my fault."

Dallas covered his sister's hands. "You aren't to blame. The kidnappers are. It's very likely you and Brady were targeted."

"How? Why?" Paul asked Dallas. "We don't have much money to pay a ransom, but we'll find a way." Paul dropped his chin against his chest. "If they ever contact us." He jerked his head up. "I guess I have to put the phone back on."

"Why don't you get one of our relatives to answer the phone for the next couple of days?" Dallas asked.

Paul frowned. "I guess I can ask my uncle. I don't think either of us can deal with the calls right now, but what if the kidnapper does call?"

"We'll trace your calls. If that's okay with you." Rachel shifted her attention from Lenora to her husband. She was worried about Dallas's sister.

"Yes, anything to bring Brady back," Lenora murmured, her words so low it was hard to understand her at first.

"Then I'll set it up, and I'll have a deputy answer the phone. Excuse me." Rachel left the room to find Deputy Jones. She wanted to give Dallas a moment to talk with his family alone. When Rachel located her deputy on the back porch, she told him about answering the phone and tracing any calls, then returned to the living room.

"Why is this happening to us?" she heard Lenora wail.

Dallas's face paled. "There are several common reasons why someone abducts a child. A familiar person like a divorced mother or father. An individual or couple who have lost a child and want to replace theirs. And people who sell babies on the black market."

And it was easier to track down a kidnapper who fit the first two motives, but she kept that observation to herself. Rachel didn't think that was the case here, which meant time wasn't on their side.

Lenora turned toward her brother. "No. This doesn't happen in Cimarron Trail. This is a safe town." Sobs tore from her, filling the air with the sound of agony.

Dallas drew her against him, his arms enveloping his sister. "I'll find Brady. I promise."

With all color bled from his face, Paul stood, opening and closing his hands. "I need to turn the phone back on. They may be calling right now with a ransom demand."

"Everything has been arranged," Rachel said while Paul charged into the kitchen.

Dallas looked at Rachel, his brown eyes darkening even more. Pain etched his expression, the hard planes of his face tearing at Rachel's composure.

Lenora leaned back and switched her attention between Rachel and Dallas while swiping her tears from her cheeks. "Y'all think he was taken to be sold."

Dallas nodded.

Rachel's chest constricted. Why, Lord? Why this baby? For the last two years of her marriage, she'd struggled to keep it together and prayed to God for an answer. The Lord never answered her call for help. She hoped He would for Lenora.

Rachel inhaled a composing breath. "Lenora, where did you go while Michelle was babysitting?"

"I went to church for a meeting about the building expansion. I'm on the committee. Then, afterwards,

I'd planned to go to the grocery store before coming home. The meeting was just ending when I got the call about Brady."

"I need a list of the people on the committee."

"None of them would take my son!"

Dallas patted Lenora's hand. "We have to check every lead possible. We aren't accusing anyone, but we wouldn't be doing our job if we didn't consider who knew you would be away from the house."

"Pastor John Wiggins, Carl Stevens, Marvin Compton and Sue Palmer." Her eyes shone with unshed tears. "They would never do something like this."

"I can't see they would either." Not even Marvin Compton, who'd run against Rachel for county sheriff.

"Please do it quietly." Lenora swiped her hand across her cheek. "I've known them for years."

"We found something I'd like you to look at." Rachel rose and closed the space between Lenora and her. She held up the bracelet in the plastic bag, making sure the heart with the initials was visible. "Do you know who this belongs to?"

Lenora's eyes grew wide. "Where did you find it?"

"In your dining room by a chair under the table."

"It's mine. Mom gave it to me a few months ago. It used to be hers, and I would play with it when I was a child. She doesn't wear it anymore, so she thought I would enjoy it."

"The initials are DN?" Rachel asked.

"Mom's maiden name was Dorothy Nash. I didn't think of that." Dallas twisted his mouth into a wry look.

Rachel took the evidence bag from Lenora and returned to the wingback. "I thought this might have been left by the kidnappers."

"It could have been." Lenora straightened. "I lost it last week when I was shopping with Brady. I looked everywhere when I realized it was gone, but I never found it."

As Paul returned to the living room after taking the portable phone out to the deputy, Rachel withdrew a pad and pen. "Where did you go that day?"

"What's going on?" Paul took his place next to his wife.

"Remember when I lost my bracelet? Rachel found it in the dining room, but it couldn't have been there. I remember having it when I left the house last week, and at the drugstore, but when I was through shopping and heading back to the car, it was gone. I retraced my steps to the last store I visited. I couldn't find it in Knit n' Pearl. Brady was so fussy I didn't go to the other two shops. I called each one and left my contact information, but no one had turned it in."

So how did it end up back at their house? Rachel had planned on showing the bracelet at the news conference tomorrow morning and asking for leads to whoever owned it. She couldn't do that now, but it was possible the woman kidnapper had found it and lost it in the dining room today. Rachel would have any prints on the piece of jewelry run through the system. "Besides Knit n' Pearl, what other places did you go to?"

"I went to two other stores in the Chesterfield Shopping Center on this side of San Antonio—Chesterfield Drug Store and Baby and Things. I normally go to the pharmacy in town, but I frequent the Chesterfield one when I shop at Knit n' Pearl and Baby and Things. We don't have anything quite like those places in Cimarron Trail."

Rachel wrote down their names. "Are the people at those stores familiar with you?"

"Knit n' Pearl, yes. I'm not sure about Baby and Things because I've only been going there for six months, after a friend told me about the store. It's a great place to buy baby clothes at a reasonable price. I doubt the cashier where I checked out in the drug store would remember me being in there." Lenora scrunched her forehead. "I don't understand. How can this help you?"

"It's possible the woman kidnapper had been following you, and when you lost your bracelet, she picked it up. I'll be interviewing the people working at those stores, and if they have any security video cameras, she might be on one of the tapes." It was the best lead they had, and after the news conference tomorrow, Rachel would go to the shopping center. "Which day and time last week did you go to the shops?"

"Friday in the morning. I left here at nine when the commuter traffic was less. It's about twenty-five minutes away."

Rachel glanced at Dallas. "Is there anything else you can think of?"

"No, not at the moment." He rose. "I wish I could stay, but I need to get back to the hospital. I still hope that Michelle will eventually remember more about what happened. There's a lot she can't recall."

Tears still in her eyes, Lenora looked up at her brother. "Please tell Michelle I don't blame her for any of this. She's a victim, too." She struggled to her feet, nearly collapsing back onto the couch.

Dallas steadied her at the same time Paul did. "I will." He enveloped his sister in a hug. "If you remember anything that might help the investigation, call me at any time of day."

Lenora nodded and eased back down onto the sofa.

"Will it be all right if the deputy stays in the house tonight? He can continue to screen your calls. If there's a ransom demand, he'll get in touch with Dallas and me right away." Although Rachel didn't think there would be a ransom demand, she was still concerned the guy in the hoodie might come back, possibly looking for the bracelet his partner wore. She was almost positive he was the male kidnapper. If the boot prints under the window and on the dirt road matched, she'd know for sure.

"Yes," Paul said.

"We'll let ourselves out." Dallas waved for Rachel to go first as they left the house. "I wish I could stay the night, but Michelle needs me."

"Not to worry. Later Deputy Owens will be relieving Ellis. He's very good at his job. Tell Michelle I hope she gets better soon." Rachel paused next to her deputy on the porch to tell him to be on the lookout for anyone hanging around the house.

"I will." Dallas descended the steps and walked toward his car. He was immediately surrounded by the five reporters waiting on the sidewalk for any tidbit of news.

Again, Rachel saw his professional facade fall into place as he dealt with the press. After Dallas's departure, she talked with Deputy Carson, then made her own way toward her vehicle, stiffening when the reporters flocked to her.

One of them stuck a microphone in her face. "Sheriff Young, what do you say to Marvin Compton's concerns about your competence to lead this investigation?"

Rachel gritted her teeth and continued toward her vehicle. She opened the driver's side door. "No comment."

Dallas entered the dimly lit hospital room to find his mother sitting next to the bed in a lounge chair that she'd moved closer to Michelle. His daughter slept.

"How're Lenora and Paul doing?" his mother whispered.

"As well as to be expected. Lenora needs you. I'm afraid she'll start blaming herself because she wasn't home when Brady was taken."

His mother pushed herself to her feet. "When Michelle was awake about an hour ago, she was doing the same. She's going to need us, too."

"Did she say anything else about the abduction?"

"No. The nurse came in to check on her, then changed her IV fluid with a new bag. After she left, Michelle and I talked a little, but every time the kidnapping came up, she started crying. I steered the conversation away from it. I could tell her head hurt, but she was trying not to say anything about it. She's always been a tough little girl."

"She's not that little anymore, Mom. She'll be fourteen soon, and before we know it, she'll be graduating from high school."

His mother gathered her purse and walked over to where he was standing. "You've been a good parent to her—both father and mother since Patricia left."

"I'm just thankful that I have you for Michelle to talk to about girl things."

"Anytime." She stood on her tiptoes and kissed his cheek. "I'll be at Lenora's if you need anything tonight."

"Thanks, Mom." He hugged her.

After she left, he took her seat next to Michelle's bed. He sighed as he tried to relax. Tomorrow would be a long day. He had to find the kidnappers before they sold Brady. And his daughter would never be safe if they were still out there, especially if they thought Michelle could ID them. He could never rest until they were found.

He closed his eyes. He didn't think he could sleep, but he'd try. He needed to, but he'd gone without much sleep while working cases before. But he didn't want to miss an important lead because he was exhausted.

As he reclined in the lounge chair, his thoughts drifted to the new sheriff. She'd grown up in Cimarron Trail, whereas he'd moved here right after Patricia left him because Lenora and Paul had settled here years before and had raved about the town. He'd wanted his daughter to have people she could turn to, especially women, and he couldn't think of anyone better than his mother and sister.

For the past three years, he'd either thrown himself into his job or spent time with his family. He hadn't had time for anything else—and certainly not another woman. In spite of his declaration, the image of Rachel Young came unbidden into his mind. Medium height with auburn hair and green eyes, there was something about her that made a man look twice. If he were totally truthful with himself, she was stunning, which immediately put him on the defensive. Patricia had been gorgeous. Men had fallen all over themselves trying to get her attention, and she'd loved it. That should have been a red flag.

In the little he'd seen of Rachel, she didn't seem like Patricia, but he didn't want to make the same mistake twice. Better to remain single and focus his life on his family and job.

As a sheriff, she appeared competent and caring. That would make working with her easier, especially if she was anything like her father. He was a good man. No wonder the county had voted for her rather than Marvin Compton, a retired police officer from Fort Worth.

"Daddy!"

Wrenched from his thoughts, Dallas shot to his feet, preparing to battle what had frightened his daughter. His eyes panned the room. No one else was there.

"Daddy, help!"

He looked toward the bed as Michelle's eyes popped open wide. Fear stared at him. "I'm right here, honey. You're okay. I won't let anyone hurt you."

Tears coursed down her cheeks. "Brady is gone."

He sat on the bed and cuddled her against himself. "I know, princess. We're looking for him."

As Michelle buried her face against him, sobs racked her body, tearing his heart into pieces. Overwhelmed with helplessness, his own eyes glistened with his sorrow.

Sucking in shaky breaths, Michelle leaned back. "You've got to find Brady, Dad. You've got to."

"I will."

She looked long and hard at him, as though measuring the truth behind his words. "I know you will." Then she laid her head against his chest.

How could he ever face his daughter if he couldn't find Brady?

Rachel carried little Katie toward the kitchen, her parents' voices drawing her to the warm, large room. Her daughter played with Rachel's hair. She laughed. "When I show up for the press conference, the reporters are going to think I didn't brush my hair, sweetie."

Katie babbled as though she were telling Rachel something important. Mama and Nana were the only words she could understand.

"I'm running late. Nana will feed you this morning, sweet pea. You be good for her and Papa." Rachel entered the kitchen with Katie continuing to chatter nonsense.

"Do you have time to sit and have breakfast?" Rachel's mother asked as she took Katie and put her in the high chair.

"No, not with the press conference in half an hour. Coffee is all I want now. I'll eat later, I promise." Rachel kissed the top of Katie's head. "Love you. I'll see you later."

"Make sure you do eat. You have to take care of yourself or you'll be no help in finding Brady."

"I know, Mom." Rachel poured coffee into a travel mug.

"You do? You were up half the night."

"How do you know?"

"I heard you pacing."

"Going over what we have right now. Like Dad knows, I'm the one in charge of this investigation."

Rachel peered at her father who rose from sitting at the table.

"I'll walk out with you," her dad said and strolled toward the back door, opening it and waiting for her to go out first.

Outside, she whirled around and faced him. "I've been in charge of cases before, but this one has implications of a baby snatching ring working in Texas and maybe even other states."

"Are you contacting the FBI?"

"Not yet. I'm working with Texas Ranger Sanders. His office has discovered other places in the state where something like this has happened in the past year. He's talking to another Texas Ranger who worked a couple of similar kidnappings in the El Paso area." Dallas had texted her this morning that Abbey Rockford would be sending him information about what they'd found in El Paso. "I also discovered that the boot prints where the escape car was parked were the same as the man who attacked me at the side of the Howards' house."

"That might help when you find the man. It's good to have a piece of evidence to place him at the scene of the crime."

"And it confirms the importance of the bracelet I found in the dining room, since the man risked coming back for it. The bracelet is the best clue we have right now."

"Good." Her dad opened the door of her vehicle. "If you need any help, let me know, but Dallas is a top-notch Texas Ranger. Listen to his instincts and advice." He hugged her. "Katie will be fine."

She gave him a smile, then slipped behind the steering wheel and left the small ranch in the foothills north of San Antonio. As she drove toward Cimarron Trail, she went over in her head what she needed to do after the press conference. A trip to Chesterfield Shopping Center. She needed a clue that led her to the couple, and if it wasn't Lenora's trip last Friday, then maybe the prints taken from the bracelet would match someone in the database.

As she reached the winding part of the two-lane highway to town, she wondered how Michelle and Dallas did last night. She doubted he got much sleep in his daughter's hospital room. She realized that she would need to talk to Michelle today, too.

She took a sharp turn, spied a spiked chain across the road and slammed on the brakes—too late. Her car rolled over the spikes and headed toward the drop off.

# FOUR

Dallas stared out of the hospital window at a new day, trying to figure out how he could be in two places at once. He didn't want to leave Michelle, but his nephew was in danger. If it truly was a baby smuggling ring, they might not stay in the area long. Time was crucial to locating Brady.

*Lord, what do I do? Where am I needed the most?*

Below he glimpsed his mother's car turning into the parking lot. She'd mentioned last night she would come back first thing this morning, but maybe she should be with Lenora. The last time he'd talked with his mother, at midnight, his sister hadn't said much to Mom or Paul. Lenora had insisted on staying up until her son was brought home. She was positive it would happen at any moment.

"Have you found Brady, Daddy?"

His daughter's soft voice interrupted his thoughts. He swung around and faced her. "No, not yet, honey, but it's been less than a day."

Tears sprang up in Michelle's eyes. "I should never have opened the door."

Dallas moved quickly to the side of her hospital

bed and took hold of her hand. "The man came into the house by the back porch door. He kicked it in. You wouldn't have been able to stop him."

"But I could have called for help sooner."

"It wouldn't have stopped the kidnapping, and you could have been injured even more than you were."

Michelle glanced around the room. "I want to leave the hospital."

"I'm sorry, but not until the doctor says it's okay. Have you remembered anything else about yesterday? Maybe about what the woman looked like?"

Her eyelids closed. "No, the blond hair is all I really noticed. It happened so fast."

The sound of the door swishing open drew Dallas's attention to his mother entering the room. Michelle's eyes popped open.

"Grandma, I'm glad to see you. Now Daddy can go find Brady. He won't leave me here alone. Can you stay?"

"Of course. That's why I'm here. Has the doctor seen you this morning?"

"No," Michelle replied, quickly followed by Dallas saying, "He won't be here until after lunch. Are you sure you're not needed at Lenora's, Mom?"

His mom squared her shoulders and fixed her gaze on Dallas. "Positive. Lenora woke me up this morning and asked me to come here to be with Michelle. The family needs you to do your job. Don't worry about us. Find Brady."

He wanted to be in both places at the same time—a father and a law enforcement officer. His ex-wife had accused him of loving his job more than his family. He didn't want his daughter to feel the same. These past three years he'd walked a tightrope between the two. But now it wasn't strangers who needed him. It was his family. "Okay, princess, but I expect your grandma to keep me informed of everything, and I'll be here to take you home from the hospital." He leaned over and kissed Michelle's cheek. "I love you."

"I love you, too, Daddy."

He grabbed his cowboy hat and set it on his head. "Mom, may I have a word with you?"

"Sweetie, I'll be right in the hallway," his mother said to Michelle, then followed him from the room.

Dallas stood in the hall across from the deputy standing guard at the door and said to his mother, "Keep trying to see if Michelle remembers anything else about the lady who came to Lenora's. Have her try to sketch her."

His mom nodded.

"And call me if there's any problems. After the press conference, there are some leads the sheriff and I are going to run down."

"What leads?"

"Sheriff Young and I are retracing Lenora's steps when she lost her bracelet last Friday. We're pursuing information about the tire tracks on the dirt road behind their house and talking to the hands at the Fowler Ranch, although according to Houston Fowler his employees don't use that back road. That gate to the ranch is usually locked." Last night Rachel had texted him about that and other pieces of information they'd discovered. "Since cattle were rustled from his ranch, the place is a fortress. I'm hoping one of his men saw something but didn't realize it."

She patted Dallas's arm. "You don't have to worry

about Michelle. No one will get to her while I'm standing guard."

That was all he needed. His mother getting hurt. "Mom, let the deputy do his job. You're with Michelle for emotional support and to ease my guilt that I'm leaving her."

"Sure, honey." She gave him a grin and a wink, then hurried back into his daughter's hospital room.

He shook his head as he left the Cimarron Trail Regional Hospital. The drive to the sheriff's office only took ten minutes. When he arrived, he pulled into the last parking space at the side of the building. Inside the station, a small crowd had already gathered. He made his way through the twenty people, some with microphones and others with cameras, like a group of sharks swarming chummed water searching for tidbits. Standing at the front was Marvin Compton, looking self-righteous, as though he'd already solved the case.

Dallas caught sight of Deputy Jones at the front, facing the reporters, and approached the chief deputy sheriff. "Where's Rachel?"

"She's not here. I called her phone, but she isn't answering."

"Where does she live?"

"With her parents on Bill's Safe Haven Ranch until she finds a place of her own."

Dallas looked over the growing crowd. "That's twenty minutes northeast of town. How's the cell reception out that way?"

"Good except for a few patchy places."

"I'll start the press conference. You try calling her again."

Dallas stepped up to the podium and waited a moment while the reporters became silent. "I'm Texas Ranger Dallas Sanders. I'm helping the sheriff's office on this investigation at the request of Sheriff Young." He told the press what little they had, and ended with, "If anyone has a lead about this case, please come forward. There is a twenty-five-thousand-dollar reward for information leading to an arrest."

Paul had called him earlier and told him he would find the money somehow if it would help bring Brady home sooner, and Dallas had promised to help him with the reward. "Please contact the sheriff's office if you have any information concerning this case. I would appreciate y'all getting the word out about the reward. Thank you for coming today." He started to step away from the podium in a barrage of questions from the reporters, but he stopped when one sounded louder than the others.

"Where is Sheriff Young? Is she shirking her job after only eleven days?"

Dallas faced the man who asked the question—Marvin Compton, the sore loser who'd lost the election for sheriff recently. The crowd quieted, sensing a confrontation, but Dallas wouldn't give the press another story instead of the kidnapping. He narrowed his gaze on Compton, waited till there was silence, then replied, "Sheriff Young, in spite of her injuries yesterday, is working diligently on the case."

Before the reporters surrounded him, Dallas marched toward the back of the station with Deputy Jones. "Did you get hold of the sheriff?" he asked quietly.

"Still no answer. I called Bill directly. He said she left over thirty minutes ago. I told him we'll check it out, that he should stay at his ranch. With this abduction yesterday, what if something happened to Katie? Rachel's number-one priority is her daughter."

"I understand. That was a good call. I'm heading out to the ranch now. I'll find her. She might have had car trouble in one of those spotty cell reception areas." Dallas hoped that was all it was. "If I need backup, I'll call you. I have a satellite phone."

"Great. We're shorthanded right now because so many are out canvassing the area around your sister's house, especially to see if anyone has security video of the street."

"Good. Let me know if anything comes of the canvass."

Dallas made his way to the station's back door and hoped the reporters didn't disperse until he'd driven out of the parking lot. He didn't want any of them following him.

As he headed out of town, he kept an eye on the cars behind him. So far it appeared he'd gotten away without a tail.

When he turned onto the two-lane highway that led to Bill's ranch, he kept his gaze sweeping from one side of the road to the other. After a few miles, he called Rachel's cell phone. Its continual ringing didn't bode well.

The constant ringing of her phone mocked Rachel's attempts to free herself from her locked seat belt while hanging upside down. She couldn't release the button on the side. She wished she was in her sheriff's cruiser, but because of budget cuts, no one could take a squad car home. In it, her location could have been tracked which would be easier than trying to track her cell phone. Although as sheriff she could have used a department vehicle, her dad hadn't done so when the decision had been made, and she had followed suit.

The ringing stopped. The scent of gasoline mingled with the dust her vehicle had stirred up. Smoke snaked from the engine. So far, she hadn't seen flames, but if a fire started...

The thought of her car exploding scared her.

Rachel gave her tight seat belt another jerk, but it didn't budge. Frustrated, she stared at her phone lying on the roof of the front passenger seat, up next to the shattered window. She leaned as far to the right as the seat belt would allow and extended her arm as far as she could toward her cell, but she was at least a foot from it.

Another call came through. Again, she tried to answer it, her sore body protesting the stretch. The belt cut into her body, making it hard to breathe. Trapped.

There had to be a way out of the car.

*Please, God, help me. Katie needs me.* The words came unbidden into her mind. She hadn't prayed in a couple of years. She'd given up on the Lord when her life fell apart, and all she'd gotten was silence.

Yet again, she yanked on the black strap. When her hand brushed against the pouch on her utility belt, she immediately knew what she needed to do. If she could get inside the bag, she could get her switchblade out. Why hadn't she thought about this ten minutes ago? She twisted to the left and fumbled for the snap. When she found it, she tugged it and it opened. She dug into the pouch and grasped the knife. As she slid her hand out, she nearly lost her grip on it. Her heart pounded double time as she clasped it safely and flicked the blade free.

Finally, she freed herself. With her dangling arms to cushion her, she fell against the roof of the car. Her left shoulder, where the seat belt had cut into her already aching body, took the brunt of the fall. She drew in deep breaths, her lungs filling with the smoky air laden with the aroma of gasoline and earth. She coughed and shifted toward her side window, a section splintered and hard to see out of. She started to slam her elbow into it when she caught sight of flames shooting out from under the hood.

Fire!

She hit the glass, pain shooting up her arm. The window remained intact.

What now?

Dallas tried again to call Rachel's cell phone, but it rang until it went to voice mail.

"Rachel, this is Dallas. Please call ASAP." He'd already left that message the last time. Frustrated, he tagged on, "Please," as though that would make a difference.

In his gut, he knew she was in trouble.

He continued his vigilant search for her as he drove toward Bill's ranch.

Boom!

Was that an explosion?

He scanned the terrain in the direction the sound had come from. A plume of smoke mushroomed into the sky, and Dallas increased his speed, a vision of Rachel in trouble driving his urgency. His heart raced. His grip on the steering wheel tightened as he came closer to the smoke rising into the sky.

*Please, Lord, protect Rachel.*

As he neared the site, he glimpsed a car in flames at the bottom of an incline. He quickly parked on the shoulder of the road, making sure his SUV was visible in both directions if someone came around the curve. After he hopped from his Jeep, he hurried to the rear and grabbed a fire extinguisher from the cargo space, then descended the slope, sliding down most of the way.

He didn't know what Rachel's personal car looked like, but he knew this was hers. He raced to the vehicle and used the fire extinguisher to spray the flames while he tried to make out the inside of the car. Coming closer to the driver's side, his pulse pounding against his temples, he spied an empty seat.

As he continued fighting the blaze, he searched the area, his gaze latching onto Rachel, with black smudges and tiny cuts on her face, rising slowly from behind a large boulder not far from her car. He finished putting out the last of the fire, then dropped the extinguisher to the ground and ran to Rachel, who had a dazed expression on her face.

"Are you all right?" All he wanted to do was wrap his arms around her and assure her he would protect her.

She wiggled her finger in her ear. "Now I am," she said in a loud voice, as though her hearing was still off.

"Where are you hurt?"

"I'm okay."

His gaze ran down her, from her messy hair to her dirty uniform, and he shouted, "Sure! You were just in a wreck and almost blown up! Unless you have secret powers I don't know about, I'd say at the very least you've been jerked around like riding a bull that tossed you up in the air and tried to gore you."

"That's a good description of how I'm feeling. Sore and bruised, but nothing broken."

"What happened?"

"I ran over a spiked chain strung across the road when I came around a curve."

"Did you see anyone?"

"No. I was trying to keep my car on the road, but it went into a spin, then plunged off the highway. I honestly don't remember much except ending up hanging upside down with a tight seat belt I couldn't release."

While Dallas withdrew his cell phone, he swept the area for any sign of life. When he noticed he had cell reception, he said, "I'm calling this in, then I'm taking you to the ER to be checked out."

"I'm fine. I can walk." She took several steps away from him.

"With a limp."

She grinned. "I was just tossed around in a car tumbling down the mountain."

"Mountain!" He laughed. "More like a small hill." He placed calls to the sheriff's office and to her father, then took pictures of the wrecked car from different angles.

She walked to the front passenger window and looked inside. "I'm going to have to buy a new cell phone. Mine was charred." She scanned the ground, walked a few feet and picked up something. "But my purse has been saved."

"Good. Ready?"

She nodded and limped to the bottom of the sixty-degree incline, then glanced back at him. "I'm going to need some help."

Moving toward her, Dallas slipped his cell phone

into his pocket, then slung his arm over her shoulders. "And I was going to ask you to help me. I slid most of the way down here."

She chuckled. "It's steep, but all I want is someone next to me in case my leg gives way."

"I can do that." He smiled down at her, feeling the warmth of her against his side. Relief shivered through him. He'd found her alive. *Thank you, Lord.*

Five minutes later, Dallas hoisted her up the last few feet, which were at an almost ninety-degree angle, onto the shoulder of the road, her body flush against his as he steadied her. For several long seconds she remained near him, sending his heart beating faster than before.

Staring into her face, he could see beads of sweat on her forehead. "Okay?"

"Yes. A shower and a fresh uniform is all I need. Can you drive me back to Dad's? It won't take me long, then we can head to Chesterfield Shopping Center."

He frowned. "With a stop first at the hospital to have a doctor check you out."

"We've already lost too much time. I'm sore but fine. If I'm still feeling bad later today, I'll let you take me to the hospital after going to the shopping center."

Instead of saying anything else, Dallas pointed toward two deputy sheriff's cars. "Backup has arrived."

After Rachel talked with Deputies Jones and Ellis about what happened, Dallas drove her to Bill's ranch, filling her in on how the press conference went. Dallas waited outside on the porch with her father, both of them sitting in rocking chairs. The view of rolling green hills with black wooden fences stretched out before Dallas.

He set his cowboy hat on his lap. "Rachel said this is more an animal sanctuary than a working ranch."

"About half and half. Deputy Rob Woodward retired when I did and finds even more animals in need of a home than I do. He lives in the small house on the other side of the barn. He helps me and in turn gets free room and board. It's been a good deal for both of us." Leaning back, Bill crossed his legs. "My daughter played down what happened to her, so tell me what's really going on. I could ask some of the deputies who used to work for me, but I don't want them to think I don't have confidence in Rachel. I do. But I didn't have a big case in the first few weeks of my job. She does, plus she has Marvin pointing out everything he thinks she's doing wrong."

"What do you think?"

"She's doing a good job. I'm trying to stay out of it, even staying away from Cimarron Trail for the time being."

"I have no complaints concerning Rachel."

Bill chuckled. "Would you tell me if you did?"

Dallas looked the retired sheriff in the eye. "Yes. She's smart, trained well and caring about the people in the county, but this case will test her." He proceeded to tell Bill the details of what had happened the previous day and earlier that morning. "I want her to go by the hospital and get checked out, but she doesn't want to waste time. She only wants to spend time tracking what few leads we have."

Bill smiled from ear to ear. "She once fell from a horse and acted like she was fine until her leg swelled up and we took her to the doctor. She has a high pain threshold, which is both good and bad. She'll let you know. She hobbled into our bedroom and woke us up in the middle of the night that time. Her determination is fierce, but she knows when to say uncle."

"Good to know. Rachel has told me about her daughter, Katie. Where is she?"

Bill gestured toward the barn. "Anita is feeding the chickens and rabbits. Katie loves to help. I'm gonna miss my granddaughter being underfoot when Rachel finds a house in town."

If someone forced Rachel off the road, what might that person do to his daughter? What was he going to do about Michelle once she left the hospital? The thought chilled Dallas in the warm summer morning air.

"But honestly, I hope Rachel isn't in too big a hurry, especially with your nephew being kidnapped. She told me it was possibly part of a statewide baby-snatching ring."

"Yeah, when I had my office look into what was happening across Texas, they discovered there were other clusters of three abductions. A Texas Ranger I know in El Paso told me when they were getting close to the kidnappers, suddenly the abductions stopped." Dallas kneaded his nape. "Now that someone's come after Rachel, I'm concerned they may be after my daughter, too. She might be able to remember what the woman looked like. She wasn't wearing a mask like the man. One of my daughter's talents is drawing, especially faces. Even with sunglasses on, she could draw the woman's face from the eyes down. That might help us."

"If you think it's a good idea, I'll watch over Michelle, too. We already look after Katie. I know my granddaughter would get a kick out of having Michelle here."

As the screen door opened, Dallas smiled. "That would work." He rose as Rachel joined them.

"What would work?" Rachel glanced from her dad to Dallas.

"Your father offered to have Michelle stay here on the ranch while we work the case."

"You think she's in danger?"

"I hope not, but I don't want to take any chances, not after your wreck today."

Bill stood. "When will she be released from the hospital?"

"Hopefully later today. Mom will let me know."

"Have Dottie call me, and we'll arrange something for today."

A huge relief came over Dallas. He couldn't ask for a better person to guard his daughter. "I don't want to put Katie at risk. Are y'all sure?"

"Yes," Rachel and Bill replied at the same time, then they looked at each other and laughed.

"Katie is already at risk. She's a baby. Ready to leave?" Rachel set her cowboy hat on her head and moved to the steps.

"Thanks." Dallas shook Bill's hand and followed her to his SUV.

Settled behind the steering wheel, he slid a look at Rachel. Her hat shadowed her face, hiding the bruises and cuts she'd sustained in the crash. From her ramrod-straight posture and the tic twitching in her jaw, he could tell she was tense. Bill was right about Rachel's fierce determination. Only an hour ago she'd had a near-death experience, and yet here she was, ready to track down any leads they had. "Do you want to stop at your crime scene before going to the shopping center?"

"No. I doubt there's any evidence to indicate who was behind the sabotage this morning. One of the few leads we have is where Lenora went on Friday. Where she lost her bracelet."

Dallas drove away from her father's house. "I agree. I hope they have surveillance cameras on the outside of the shopping center and in the stores, too."

Rachel sighed as she reclined. "Your sister went to the drugstore first, then the baby shop and finally the knitting one. Where did she park?"

"I don't know. Let me call her." Dallas quickly got in touch with Lenora. "Where did you park at the shopping center?"

"In front of the Knit n' Pearl. Are you there now?"

"Not yet. Did you remember anything else since yesterday?"

"I know I had it on in the drugstore but didn't when I left the Knit n' Pearl."

"Thanks, sis," he said, even though she'd already told him yesterday. "I'll keep you informed of our progress on the case."

"Please, just bring my baby home." The last word came out on a sob.

"I'll do all I can." When Dallas disconnected his cell phone, the sound of pain in his sister's voice lingered in his mind. What if his best wasn't enough?

"You okay?" Rachel's soft voice reminded Dallas he couldn't let self-doubt take hold.

He nodded. "Let's retrace my sister's steps the best we can, even though we're here two hours later than she was last Friday." He'd worked enough abduction cases that were never solved to be concerned. In a kidnapping case, time was of the essence, especially the first twenty-four hours—which was quickly running out for Brady. How was he going to face Lenora if he couldn't find his nephew?

# FIVE

Rachel straightened in the front passenger seat as Dallas pulled into the Chesterfield Shopping Center, which had a row of six stores facing seven other stores across the parking lot. She noticed the Baby and Things sat next to the Chesterfield Drug Store. Knit n' Pearl was across from them. Dallas parked in a spot in front of the tax accounting firm next door.

"I only see one video camera at the end of the sidewalk." He pointed to the left.

"I wonder if it belongs to the store it's in front of or the company that owns this center."

"When we're through, we'll ask, although I think the butcher shop put it up. I don't see any outside cameras at the other end."

"Nor in the parking lot. Not a lot of security. I'd be curious how much crime takes place here."

Dallas started across the parking lot. "The houses around this area are nice—middle to upper end. Maybe crime is low in this part of San Antonio." At the drugstore, he held the door open for Rachel.

A young girl with a long ponytail, probably no older than twenty, worked behind the cash register. When she looked at them, the teenager's eyes widened when they fixed on Dallas. Rachel leaned close and whispered, "I have a feeling you'll get more from her than I would. I'm going to walk around the store and see what kind of security they have."

Smiling, Dallas approached the checkout and tipped his cowboy hat. Rachel didn't hear what he said to the cashier but glimpsed him showing her the photo of Lenora. As Rachel circled the store, she noted four security cameras and paused in the rear at the pharmacy. "Is the manager here?" she asked the older woman behind the counter.

"He should be."

"Where can I find him?"

"I'll call him."

"Thanks." While the woman made an announcement asking Mr. Matthews to come to the pharmacy, Rachel turned toward the rows of merchandise. When the older lady finished, Rachel swung back to her, holding up a photo of Lenora. "Do you remember seeing this woman here last Friday morning, probably around ten?"

"I can't help you. I don't come in until eleven." The pharmacy tech stared at Rachel's sheriff's badge. "Is there a problem?"

"This woman lost a bracelet here last Friday."

"Must be an expensive bracelet if you're here checking on it."

Rachel glimpsed a man in his thirties with a name badge pinned to his shirt coming toward them. She pivoted and held out her hand. "Mr. Matthews, I'm Sheriff Rachel Young. Thanks for meeting with me."

"What's this about?"

"I'm investigating a kidnapping case." She moved farther away from the counter and lowered her voice. "I see you have surveillance cameras throughout the store and one outside near the entrance. I'm interested in video footage from Friday between 9:30 a.m. to 12:00 noon."

"Was there a kidnapping here at the store?"

"No, but a piece of evidence related to this case may have been lost in your store." When the man didn't say anything, Rachel noticed Dallas making his way toward them. From the solemn expression on his face, she could tell he hadn't found anyone who remembered Lenora. "An eight-month-old baby was kidnapped. The family is devastated."

The manager paled. "We keep security tapes for a month. I'll help any way you need. I heard on the news about an abduction in Cimarron Trail. Is that it?"

She nodded. "Mr. Matthews, this is Texas Ranger Dallas Sanders. He's working with me on the case."

Dallas shook the manager's hand. "We appreciate any help you can give us."

"Come back to my office, and I'll get you the surveillance footage from Friday. All the cameras in the store were working, but the one outside went down Friday morning. Nothing was taped on it. I didn't realize until later in the afternoon. We don't monitor them all the time, but throughout the day, I'll glance at them."

"What happened to the camera outside?"

"Someone sprayed its lens. In fact, some of the other stores said the same thing happened to their outside cameras."

"Did any footage catch the person spraying the lens?"

"Mine didn't. I think Baby and Things might have.

You need to check with them." The manager moved toward a door at the back of the store.

Mr. Matthews ran the surveillance tape on his computer to make sure it was what they wanted, fast forwarding through the first twenty minutes until it showed a woman pushing a baby carriage into the store.

Dallas tapped the screen. "That's the woman."

Mr. Matthews copied the footage onto a flash drive.

A few minutes later, Rachel and Dallas left and headed to the Baby and Things shop next door.

When Rachel stepped inside and looked around the large open space filled with every item a baby might need, she whistled. "Now I understand why Lenora drives over here. I could do some serious damage in this place."

Dallas smiled. "Let's show Lenora's picture to the employees."

"Did you notice when we came in, the camera lens outside is still painted black?"

"Yeah, whereas Mr. Matthews had a new lens. That'll be a good question to ask the manager."

Rachel took the right side of the store while Dallas canvassed the left. The first salesperson she met studied the photo Rachel showed her and couldn't help her. Rachel moved on to the next employee.

"Have you seen this woman shopping in this store recently?"

The older woman cocked her head. "She looks familiar. I've seen her somewhere, but I can't tell you where or when. I forget people's names, but I remember faces."

"But you can't say she was in here last Friday morning?"

"No. I was off that day. You need to talk with Carrie Zoeller and Lynn Davis. They worked on Friday."

"Where are they?" Rachel scanned the shop and caught sight of Dallas speaking to a middle-aged man with blond hair at the rear of the store.

"They don't work on Tuesday. They both work Thursday, Friday and Saturday. We're closed on Sunday."

"Who else was here on Friday who is working right now?"

"Our owner." The older lady waved toward Dallas and the blond-headed man. "The young girl at checkout and Betty Biden, who you just talked to."

Rachel withdrew her business card and gave it to the salesperson. "If you remember where you've seen this woman, please give me a call. This involves a kidnapping case and time is critical."

"Oh, my! Now I remember where I've seen her. On the news this morning on TV. I've waited on her before but not Friday."

"Thanks."

Before joining Dallas, Rachel hurried toward the cashier with beautiful long red hair at the back counter. Rachel noted her name on the badge she wore: Jan Thomas. "I understand you were working last Friday morning. Did you see this woman in here pushing a baby stroller?"

"Yes. She bought some clothes for her son. He was so adorable. In fact, later I remember she called the store to see if anyone had found an antique bracelet with a gold heart with the initials DN engraved on it. She'd lost it but wasn't sure where."

"Did you find a bracelet like that?"

"No, but I remembered seeing it when she was paying for her purchases, so she didn't lose it in here."

"Did anyone help her in the store?"

"Yes, Carrie did. She's not working today." Her eyebrows slashed downward. "Is the woman in trouble? She was so nice."

"She isn't, no. This is about a kidnapping case."

"The baby in the stroller?"

Rachel nodded.

Jan gasped and shook her head. "I can't believe that. If I remember anything else, I'll let you know."

"Thanks." Rachel wound her way through the store to join Dallas and the owner, Steve Tucker.

"I'm sorry we don't have any security tapes for you. We don't keep them past two days unless there's an issue that we might need the tape."

"Thanks," Dallas said. "I appreciate the list of the people who worked on Friday and their contact information."

"I wish I could help you more. I didn't arrive at the store until one on Friday."

When they exited the shop, Rachel glanced up at the black lens. "Why doesn't he have the outside camera fixed yet?"

"He told me he hadn't gotten around to it, but he showed me the brief glimpse of who blacked out the lens. He'd made a photo of him before erasing the tape. All I saw was a face with a ski mask on—black. Sound familiar?"

"The guy who attacked Michelle."

Dallas drew in a long breath. "It'll be a pleasure to bring this guy in."

Rachel gently fingered her bruised, sore face. "If he's the guy who hit me—and the evidence seems to indicate that—I'll be right there next to you."

"Let's check Knit n' Pearl out. So far, not much to go on."

"The cashier, Jan Thomas, told me she saw Lenora wearing her bracelet when she paid for her purchases. That narrows down when she could have lost it."

Dallas frowned. "In the Knit n' Pearl shop or somewhere out here, most likely."

"Lenora went back to the Knit n' Pearl. She didn't find it."

"So, this is where we need to concentrate." He swung the door to the shop open and waited for Rachel to go in.

When she entered, a warm and fuzzy feeling immediately enveloped her as she moved farther inside. Several round tables off to one side were filled with women and one man, knitting. A lady, probably about sixty with salt-and-pepper hair, moved from one person to the next, assisting and encouraging the knitters. Laughter filled the air that was scented with lavender and vanilla.

"I've never thought about learning to knit, but this place makes it tempting to try. I'll talk with the lady helping at the tables." Rachel glanced around the cozy shop. "It doesn't look like they have many cameras."

"I'll see what the lady behind the counter says."

As Rachel approached the two tables, the chatter subsided. Most stared at their knitting projects while their hands slowed. A couple followed her progress. Rachel stopped next to the instructor and lowered her voice. "May I talk with you for a few minutes?"

"This is about Lenora Howard and Brady's kidnapping?"

Rachel nodded. "You're following the story?"

"Yes. She's been a good customer for a while. The last time I saw her was Friday."

"I'm Sheriff Rachel Young."

When she held out her hand, the older woman shook it. "I'm Barbara Norris, the owner of this shop."

"I understand Lenora lost a bracelet and came back in here to look for it."

"Yes. Me and Annie, my sister and partner in the shop, helped her to look around the store at that time. She was so upset about losing it."

"It was a gift from her mother."

Barbara stared off to the left of Rachel. "I hated seeing tears in Lenora's eyes. We searched everywhere, even after she was gone. Brady started crying and nothing she did calmed him so she left. I told her I would call her if we found it."

"How many customers did you have when Lenora was here?"

Barbara tapped her finger against her jaw. "There were five people browsing the merchandise. Two helped us look for the bracelet."

"Do you know who the customers were?"

"The two who searched with us were regulars—Donna Eagan and her daughter, Linda. The other ones I didn't know. They looked around and left. A young woman with a man who seemed uncomfortable being in our store and a gray-haired woman."

When Rachel noticed Annie hand Dallas something and he turned to leave, she gave Barbara her card. "If you remember anything else about that day, please let me know."

"Ready?" Dallas asked Rachel.

"Yeah." She headed for the exit and started to push the door open.

Instead, Dallas leaned around her and thrust it wide. His soft touch at the small of her back shivered down her spine. She slanted a look at him, his lime-scented aftershave wafting in the air between them. For a long second, their gazes connected. Her breath caught while her pulse raced.

Dallas cleared his throat and glanced away. "When we get in the car, I want you to use my computer to look at the footage from the Knit n' Pearl."

His words brought her back to the moment. She blinked and quickly stepped outside into the hot summer day. What in the world had happened back there? Rachel tried to make sense of that brief interaction between them.

As she settled into the front passenger seat, Dallas picked up his laptop and loaded the footage from the thumb drive onto it, then he passed it to Rachel.

"I hope there's something on the video because we don't have many leads." She focused her full attention on what was playing out on the screen.

The sisters at the knitting shop didn't have many security cameras, but what they had gave a clear view of almost the whole place. When she found something she wanted to explore more closely, she stopped the black and white video and zoomed in, especially when she glimpsed the bracelet was no longer around Lenora's wrist. Rachel zoomed out wide but kept her gaze on the spot where the piece of jewelry sat on the floor near a large basket of multicolored skeins.

As Lenora picked up a crying Brady and tried to comfort him, a young woman with long light-colored hair and wearing sunglasses stopped by the basket of yarns. When the lady stood, sliding her hand into her jeans pocket, Rachel fixed her gaze on the spot where the bracelet had been.

Empty.

"I found the woman!"

Dallas swerved off the highway onto the shoulder and parked. "Let me see."

Rachel rewound the video, then gave the laptop to him. "The lady conveniently has her face turned away from the cameras. So does the man with her. That's not a coincidence. I traced her from when she came in, and I can't find one good shot of her face."

"Although the video is black and white, it appears her hair is light colored, likely blond. We need to get a good drawing of the lady at Lenora's house. I'll call Annie later and see if she'll try to describe the woman for a sketch artist."

"How about Michelle? She might recognize her if she's shown the illustration."

"First, I want her to try without any reference from the people at Knit n' Pearl. If she can do a drawing, we can compare it with what the two sisters come up with."

Rachel took back the laptop as Dallas started the engine and pulled onto the highway to Cimarron Trail. "Lenora needs to see this footage. She may remember something about the woman and man."

At a four-way stop sign, Dallas called Knit n' Pearl, then his office and had a sketch artist go to the knitting shop. "After that, have him call me, and I'll meet him at my sister's house." After disconnecting, he crossed the intersection, only ten minutes away from Cimarron Trail.

As he hit the outskirts of the town, a call came in from his mother. He pulled off the road to answer it. "I just returned from San Antonio. Is Michelle leaving the hospital soon?"

Rachel couldn't tell what his mother replied but thought the smile on his face must mean good news. She hoped so. She could imagine how she would feel if something happened to her daughter.

When he ended the call, he continued toward the regional hospital and pulled into the parking lot. "Michelle has drawn a picture of the lady who forced herself into Lenora's house yesterday."

"Great. Will she be able to leave the hospital?"

"Yes. Mom said she was doing better in the past couple of hours."

Having been hit like Michelle by the Peeping Tom, although not as seriously hurt as the teenager, Rachel was relieved to hear she was improving. The whole affair was terrifying, especially for a young girl. Her heart went out to Michelle. "Not only do I think that Michelle should stay at my dad's ranch while we're investigating this case, I think she should stay there rather than going back and forth between your home and my father's place. She needs to rest and relax. You both should stay there until this is all over. It'll give us more time to work on the case in the evening."

He switched off his SUV and turned toward her. "I appreciate Bill offering to protect Michelle while we're investigating, but—"

"Dad's house is large. Plenty of room for y'all. We should stick together. If Brady's kidnapping is connected to the other ones in Texas recently, then we're up against a well-organized group. Have you found out from your office about any similar kidnappings in other states?"

"Not yet. I agree about us facing an organization that has deep pockets. Let's go rescue Michelle from the hospital."

As Rachel hopped down from the SUV, she chuckled. "That's how I would feel."

"Me, too." Across the hood, Dallas's look captured hers. "We'll catch all of them. Don't worry."

In that moment, she felt the total conviction behind each of his words. A real smile took over her face. "If I have anything to do with it, yes. I can't let anything I do fuel Marvin's rhetoric about me being the sheriff."

Dallas headed inside. "I support that one hundred percent."

As Rachel climbed the stairs to the second floor, despite the aches and pains she had from the car accident earlier, there was a lightness to her step. Dallas's support meant a lot to her. She was a responsible law enforcement officer, but she could also recognize when she needed help with a case. Kidnapping babies from their parents was horrendous but selling them was even worse. And she was determined to stop this smuggling ring. No matter what.

Dallas emerged from Bill Young's house onto the front porch just as the sun was disappearing behind the hills to the west. "It was nice to see you again, Rob." Dallas shook the hand of Rob Woodward, a former deputy who now worked and lived at the ranch.

"Anytime I can help y'all, just holler. I ain't letting

anyone hurt little Katie or Michelle." Rob stuck his pinkie up. "Katie's got me wrapped around her finger. One smile and I melt."

"I appreciate you offering to keep an eye out for anything unusual and to show Michelle around the ranch once the doctor says it's okay for her to resume her activities. She loves horses."

"Speaking of horses, I need to check on Sunshine. She hasn't been eating." Rob descended the steps and tipped his cowboy hat, then sauntered in the direction of the barn.

Dallas leaned into the wooden railing that surrounded the porch, taking in a deep breath of the grass-scented air. This was his favorite time of day, as the sun went down and darkness crept over the landscape. He'd hoped to have some time to spend with his daughter, but right after dinner she'd gone to bed early. He wasn't surprised because there had been so many people coming and going from the hospital room that she'd hardly rested.

The screen door opened, and he glanced over his shoulder—at Rachel. A smile curved her full lips and reached deep into her crystal-green eyes. She made him forget—for just a few moments—they weren't in the middle of an abduction case involving his nephew with his daughter the only witness.

"Did Katie go to bed?" Dallas turned and leaned against the railing.

"Yes. Michelle wore her out. Katie put her head down and went right to sleep."

"My daughter loves children. Brady always responds…" The rest of what he was going to say caught in his throat. He'd promised his sister he would bring

Brady home, and yet he knew the longer it took, the less likely it was that he would.

"Is she still blaming herself?"

"She won't talk about it anymore. I thought Mom could get her to open up. But she couldn't." He crossed his legs and gripped the railing while Rachel stood right in front of him. "I'm worried. When my wife left us and signed over full custody to me, Michelle was silent. Even when I found her crying, she wouldn't talk to me. Slowly she's begun to open up, but now…" he shook his head "…I don't know what to do."

Rachel reached out and clasped his arm. "It's not easy being a teenage girl. She's caught between being a child and an adult. She was—and is—scared. I tend to clam up when I'm afraid, too."

The vulnerability behind her last sentence touched his own. When you cared about someone, you left yourself open to be hurt. Patricia's leaving him and Michelle had hurt him more than he'd thought possible. Somehow he'd missed the signs that she was unhappy. He'd been trained to read people and try to figure out what they were thinking. But Patricia had fooled him up until the day she'd walked out after serving him the divorce papers. He would never let that happen to him again.

He stared at the darkening terrain, at the countless stars in the midst of the black sky. "We should go inside. No sense making it easy to get to us."

"You think you're in danger, too?" She moved closer to him and scanned the yard.

"Prepare for the worst. That way we won't be surprised again, like what happened to you this morning."

"I'll be creeping around that curve at five miles an hour from now on."

He looked down at her, the light of the porch was behind her, shadowing her features, but from the tone of her voice he imagined there was a twinkle in her eyes. "We should be extra vigilant."

"As you say, prepare for the worst. Good motto for any law enforcement officer." Rachel walked to the door and went inside.

Dallas took one last look at the ranch. He couldn't shake the sensation that someone lurked out there in the darkness, watching. Other than his mother, he hadn't told anyone that he and Michelle were staying here. He hoped it was his imagination or the result of his talk with Rachel, but he couldn't dismiss the eerie feeling.

Standing in the entry hall, he made sure the front door was locked. He'd already checked the windows, even the second floor ones. Rachel must have gone to the den where they had set up a laptop to go through any evidence they acquired concerning the case.

As he passed the living room, Rachel's mother, sitting next to her husband, said, "I made a pot of coffee for you and Rachel in case you need it."

Bill put down the book he was reading. "How about me? I'm going to be up part of the night."

Anita looked back and forth between her husband and Dallas. "You think they'll come to the ranch?"

"Hopefully not, but I don't want to take a chance." Bill patted her leg. "Rob's coming back to take the early morning watch. We're splitting it three ways, so we'll all get some sleep."

Anita twisted her mouth into a frown. "You're right.

They tried to kill Rachel earlier. If you're on duty later, you need to get some sleep right now. The people we love are in this house."

Bill gave his wife a quick kiss and rose. "Yes, ma'am." As he passed Dallas, he added. "I'm setting my alarm for midnight. I want you to get enough rest so you can solve this crime quickly."

Dallas nodded, continuing toward the den. He leaned in through the doorway. "Do you want a cup of coffee?" he asked Rachel.

Rachel shook her head. "I'm fine. We don't have a lot of leads yet. I'll probably call it a night soon. My aches and bruises are protesting. I'm not even sure I can get up," she said with a chuckle.

"Actually, we can do that tomorrow morning if you want, right before we go back to the Chesterfield Shopping Center. That may be a better time, anyway." Dallas moved closer and held his hand out.

She took it and allowed him to pull her up, her eyes trained on his. "Thanks."

"I've been in your shoes before. If you sit too long, you get stiff." He should've stepped back, but her beautiful face transfixed him, demanding he move even closer.

He wondered what it would feel like if he kissed her. Ever since Patricia had left him, he'd stayed focused on his job and family, not allowing anyone to distract him from those two things. But now, the urge to brush her mouth with his overwhelmed him. He bent his head toward hers.

Kiss me floated through her mind as Rachel stood frozen in front of Dallas. Would she shock him if she put her arms around his neck and drew him even closer? Her cheeks flushed. But before she could act on impulse, he hooked his arm around her waist and gently tugged her against him while his mouth settled on hers.

For a few, brief seconds.

Then he pulled back, his eyes fluttering open. Surprise flitted across his face. "I'm sorry. I shouldn't have done that."

"I'm glad you did," Rachel said. "When I discovered that my husband had a mistress at the time of his death, my world was rocked. It made me doubt everything I believed in. He'd betrayed me, and yet I questioned myself, going over and over what I had done wrong, asking myself why he would do that to me."

"Was he a police officer?"

"No, an accountant. He'd never asked me about my work, and I was okay about that. When I left work, I put the day's activities behind me. I didn't want to burden him with some of the things I saw on the job."

One corner of his mouth tilted up. "I did the very same thing, but because Patricia asked me not to share. So I kept it inside."

"Thankfully when I was really troubled, Dad was there to listen. We all need someone to talk to when we're upset."

"I'm glad you have your father. I have a couple of buddies. We share war stories when we get together. One is Taylor Blackburn. He's a Texas Ranger who works in the San Antonio office and I've asked him to help with the case. He's great at digging up information online." Dallas stepped back. "You need to get some rest. Today has been challenging. I'm surprised you didn't go to your bedroom when Michelle did."

"My mistake was when I finally sat down in here a few minutes ago."

"I'll take a look at the footage and write down anything that concerns me. Tomorrow morning we'll see if we agree."

Tonight she'd gotten to know Dallas on a deeper level. She'd never talked about her marriage with anyone, especially someone she'd just met. She felt like she'd known him longer than a couple of days. "Make sure you get some rest, too." As she strolled out of the den, she glanced back at him before he disappeared from view.

The image of his head bowed and his shoulders hunched made her step falter. She reached out and put her hand on the hallway's wall. Was he thinking about his ex-wife? She knew what it felt like to be devastated by betrayal. The urge to go back and make him realize Patricia walked out on him—not the other way around—was strong.

Rachel stopped at the upstairs bathroom to wash her face and brush her teeth. When she was finished and heading down the corridor to her bedroom, she passed by Michelle's room. The sound of a moan stopped Rachel in her tracks. Was something wrong? She moved closer to the door to listen.

Suddenly a scream shrieked through the air.

# SIX

Rachel burst into Michelle's room, preparing herself to do battle with whoever was in there. The light from the hallway spotlighted the bed, where the young teen sat straight up, her hands clutching the sheet. Rachel hurried toward Michelle, who slowly looked in Rachel's direction, the girl's eyes round as full moons.

As Rachel sat next to Michelle, the teen shivered. Rachel gathered her into her arms and drew Michelle against her. "Just a bad dream. You're all right now. I won't let anyone hurt you."

"I saw her." Michelle clung to Rachel as if she were drowning and was trying to stay above water.

"Who?"

The young girl mumbled something. The only words Rachel heard clearly were "the woman."

"What woman?" she asked Michelle.

"The lady who took Brady."

At that moment, something blocked the light from the hallway. Rachel slanted a look toward the door and saw Dallas quickly enter the room.

As he sat nearby on the bed, Rachel shifted her focus back to Michelle and said, "What about the lady?"

"I knocked her sunglasses off."

Rachel exchanged a glance with Dallas. "Do you remember what she looked like without her glasses?"

The teenager nodded. "She'd picked up Brady. I was trying to stop her."

"What happened next?" Dallas asked in a soft voice as he placed a hand on his daughter's shoulder.

She looked at her father. "I tried to get Brady away from her. That was when I was hit. I should have been able to save him. I should have…" Tears glistened in her eyes.

"Honey, there was nothing you could have done."

The tightness in his voice battered at Rachel's composure. She knew exactly what he was going through—he felt helpless to change what happened.

"I shouldn't have opened the door to her. If Brady dies…" Her sobs whisked away the rest of the sentence as she clung to her father.

"He won't. We'll find him, I promise, honey." Dallas's gaze locked with Rachel's.

In his eyes, she glimpsed a father fighting desperately to reassure his child. But it was something he had no control over and he knew that. Hope was wonderful, but what would happen when he couldn't fulfill his promise?

"Let's pray for Brady, princess."

Rachel frowned. Praying hadn't helped her. If that was what he depended on, he might be disappointed. She'd prayed after Justin died to help her get through the pain, but instead she'd discovered he'd been having an affair for a year. The knowledge had left her devastated, with more questions and no hope of answers.

"Daddy, I have been."

"Good. We'll do it together. There are never too many prayers."

Michelle nodded.

As Dallas and his daughter bowed their heads, Rachel left them to pray alone. She didn't want to dampen their hope, but praying didn't guarantee anything.

She hurried to her room and finished getting ready for bed, her hands shaking as she buttoned her pajama top. Too keyed up to sleep, she sat in a chair, her teeth chewing on her bottom lip. She didn't want Dallas or Michelle to be hurt even more when God let them down. The anger she experienced when she thought of her late husband welled up inside her. She'd worked hard not to think about him and now that seemed to be all she was doing.

She massaged her temples as though that action would drive him from her mind. But one of the texts she'd seen on his cell phone pushed everything else from her thoughts: *I'm asking Rachel for a divorce tomorrow. Promise.*

Those words haunted her, even fifteen months later.

Forget it.

But she couldn't.

A light knock brought her back to the present. She slipped on a robe and quickly answered the door, welcoming any distraction from what she couldn't change.

"How's Michelle?" she asked Dallas, noting his arms straight at his sides, his hands curling then uncurling.

"Okay. I told her she was safe now. She described the woman with light weird eyes that were big and round. I'm not sure if that will help, but she'll update her drawing tomorrow. I told her the drawing was very important to our investigation. It seemed to make her feel better."

"Good. If she wakes up again, I'll hear her. I'm a light sleeper."

"Thanks for being there for her, Rachel."

"Any time. Katie has already fallen in love with Michelle in the short time your daughter has been here."

"I think the feeling is mutual." He smiled, his eyes softening, his stance relaxing. "Good night."

"Make sure you get some rest. We have a long day ahead of us tomorrow."

Rachel shut her door and leaned against it, her heart thumping against her rib cage. The memory of his kiss brought instant heat to her cheeks. She was surprised at such a reaction. She understood where he was coming from. Their jobs were tough, and not having someone to share that with was hard on a law enforcement officer. She pictured his smile and the warm look in his eyes. She shivered—in a good way. Could she ever trust a man again? Even one like Dallas?

She made her way to the bed. When she lay down and closed her eyes, an image of Justin leaving popped into her head. His last words to her rang through her mind: *I don't want to be the father of your child.*

Those words still cut deep into her heart, shattering her dreams of what she'd wanted from their marriage. She didn't know how to heal from that kind of rejection, and she certainly didn't want to go through that again.

Was she willing to put herself through all that pain again?

* * *

The next morning, Dallas came down the stairs, pleased that he'd managed to get six hours of sleep. Rob, wearing a holster and gun, stood in the living room watching out the large window. At six in the morning the house was still quiet.

"Any problems?" Dallas asked Rob.

The retired deputy sheriff looked at Dallas. "Not a peep."

"That's what I like to hear."

"I thought you'd sleep later."

"You know how a case can be. Too much crammed in my head, demanding attention. Since I'm up now, you don't have to stay and guard the house."

"I'm gonna go feed the animals, then take a nap. Getting old ain't for the faint of heart."

Dallas chuckled and headed for the kitchen to put coffee on to brew. Before coming downstairs, he'd peeked into Michelle's room and was glad to see her sleeping. He hoped that their prayers last night had helped her begin to deal with her guilt. His daughter wasn't to blame, but that was hard for anyone, let alone a teenager, to understand. He didn't want her to let guilt overtake her life.

After he poured himself a cup of coffee, he made his way to the den. When he stepped into the room, he found Rachel watching the footage on the laptop.

She paused the video and glanced at him. "You look rested."

"I am. That's what sheer exhaustion will do to a person. I don't think I slept a wink the night before."

"Hospitals will do that to you. I'm glad to see Michelle is still sleeping. But I have to admit, I can't wait until she gets up and redoes her drawing of the woman. We need to take the updated version with us to the shopping center."

Dallas placed his mug on the table. "Before I get settled, would you like some coffee?"

She looked up at him, her face glowing from the obvious rest she'd gotten last night. "Yes, half milk and a spoonful of sugar."

"You mean your milk is flavored with the coffee?" He grinned.

"Yes." She eyed his mug. "I don't know how you can drink it black."

He sauntered toward the hallway, saying, "I'm a simple kind of guy."

"Milk and sugar aren't what I consider fancy," she called out as he left.

His smile grew as he entered the kitchen. It was easy to talk with Rachel. Since Patricia left him he hadn't dated anyone. His job and his daughter had demanded all his time, or at least, that was the excuse he gave himself when his friends had tried to fix him up with women. But with Rachel, it was fun teasing and bantering back and forth with her. He'd missed that.

He should regret the kiss they'd shared last night—it had been unprofessional in the middle of a case. But he didn't regret it one bit. He hadn't felt this way in a long time, but he was smart and cautious enough to realize he needed to take things slow.

When he reentered the den and sat next to Rachel, the scent of vanilla drifted to him, mocking his cautious side. "Any revelations from watching the security footage again?"

"No, other than the sisters at Knit n' Pearl got a

good view of the woman who later took the bracelet. Between them, hopefully we'll get a confirmation of what the lady looks like. If we find her, we'll most likely find her male accomplice."

"That's what I was thinking. I didn't see anyone who looked even remotely like her at the drugstore, and since there weren't any security tapes from Baby and Things, we can't say anything about that place."

"But we should take the drawings from the sisters and Michelle to that shop. Maybe one of them will trigger a memory."

"We'll stop by your station to get the sketch artist's illustrations. Plus, we need to visit the other workers that weren't at the store yesterday but were working when my sister went in."

"You think the team was stalking Lenora?" Rachel closed the laptop and relaxed back in her chair while sipping her coffee.

"Possibly. Maybe they followed her home and tried to figure out when the best time was to take Brady."

"Morning! How long have you two been up?" Rachel's father asked from the den's entrance.

"Half an hour," Dallas answered.

"An hour." Rachel rose. "I should probably check on Katie. She's usually awake by now."

"If she is, she's being extra quiet."

"That's when I worry. She can get into trouble faster than a cheetah."

Bill came into the room as Rachel left. "Any leads?"

"Yes. Michelle remembered something last night. She knocked the sunglasses off the woman's face and saw what she looked like without them." Dallas took another sip of coffee. "I wonder if she's awake yet. I'm tempted to go upstairs and see."

"You don't need to. As I came downstairs, I spied her going into the guest bathroom on the second floor. She'll be down soon, especially when Anita starts cooking breakfast."

"Good. We'll be going to the shopping center again today with what we know about the lady kidnapper." Out of the corner of his eye, Dallas caught sight of his daughter entering the room. "We were just talking about you, princess." He stood and hugged her. "Did you sleep all right?"

"Yes. I want to work on the drawing. Where's my first one?"

Dallas reached across the table and snatched up her illustration. "I'd like you to do a new one. Okay?"

Nodding, Michelle took the sketchpad and sat on the other side of the table.

"I'll be right back. I want to get some more coffee. Do you want anything to drink?"

She shook her head, never looking up.

Dallas walked with Bill into the hallway. "She gets into a zone when she draws. The artist we use texted me last night, and said he didn't get much from the sisters at the Knit n' Pearl, so I'm not sure how detailed his pictures will be. According to him, each description the sisters gave was very different, but if they see a picture Michelle drew, they might recognize the woman."

"What I think is strange is the outside cameras weren't working."

"I agree, but every time they're fixed they're taken out. It could be kids playing pranks or something more sinister. If I can find a good place for it, I'm putting up a small surveillance camera for the parking lot. I've got an idea that might work, at least for a few days."

One of Bill's eyebrows lifted. "My curiosity is piqued."

"There's a billboard near the parking lot. I'm having one mounted up on it."

When Dallas and Bill entered the kitchen, they spotted Rachel's mother standing at the stove flipping pieces of bacon. Dallas crossed the room and refilled his mug. "That smells wonderful."

"I'm fixing a big breakfast. I know my daughter will most likely skip lunch. She always does when she's on a case."

Dallas laughed. "I'm guilty of doing the same thing." The aroma of baking mingled with the scents of coffee and bacon. "Are you making biscuits, too?"

Anita nodded. "With gravy and scrambled eggs."

"Michelle is going to be spoiled. At our house breakfast is usually a bowl of cereal."

Anita grinned. "Just Michelle?"

"No, me, too. Cooking isn't my forte. That's why my daughter is cooking more and more."

"Michelle. She likes to cook." Anita looked from Rachel to Dallas. "So does Rachel. In fact, I could use your help if Bill will take Katie. You can make the scrambled egg mixture."

Bill stood by the back door. "First I need to check in with Rob before he heads to town later."

"I'll take Katie." Dallas covered the distance to Rachel, holding his arms out for the baby. "Katie, we'll go find Michelle. Okay?"

"Mimi." Katie launched herself into Dallas's embrace.

"So that's what my daughter calls Michelle. She's been jabbering that name while I was dressing her. That's one mystery solved." Rachel approached her mother.

"Let's hope the others are that easy." Dallas settled Katie against him and headed for the den. "We're going to Mimi."

Katie looked up at Dallas with the same green eyes as her mother. "Mimi. Mimi."

When Dallas found Michelle finishing her drawing, Katie leaned toward his daughter with her arms outstretched.

"You have a visitor."

Michelle's whole face lit up with a huge smile. "Katie!" Scooting the chair back, she took the young girl from Dallas. "I'm glad you're up. Remember you're showing me the barn and animals today." She rose with the baby in her arms, nodding at her sketch. "That's what the woman looked like to me. I only saw her for a few seconds, but her eyes were light gray—almost silver. Hard to forget."

"Thanks, honey. I know this was difficult for you, but it'll help us find the kidnappers," Dallas said as Katie played with Michelle's long hair.

"I hope so."

"When are you going to the barn?" He didn't want her to go, especially with Katie, without someone else being there, too.

"Katie's papa is taking us. When the doctor says it's okay, Bill said I could ride one of his horses."

"That's fine, I just don't want you to leave the house alone."

Michelle's eyes darkened. "I won't, I promise. Besides, someone has to be here to play with this sweet thing. Isn't that right?" she asked Katie.

Katie threw her arms around Michelle's neck as the pair moved into the hallway.

Dallas stayed behind to look at his daughter's drawing. With the sunglasses gone, the picture indicated the woman had high cheekbones and dark eyebrows and lashes. She might have been wearing a blond wig. He'd have Michelle produce another illustration with dark hair and use both when he went back to the shopping center.

For the first time in thirty-eight hours, he felt they had a good chance to find the kidnappers, and possibly Brady.

"When things settle down, I plan on coming back here to shop at Baby and Things. Yesterday I saw some darling clothes for Katie." Rachel slipped out of Dallas's SUV, parked in front of Knit n' Pearl. She met Dallas on the sidewalk. "Katie loves being with Michelle."

"Yeah, and Michelle is loving that. Katie has been good for my daughter since the kidnapping."

"She's very good with children. A natural."

Dallas opened the door to the shop and waited until Rachel went inside, then followed. "I'm glad we got here early before their knitting classes started. I want them to see the video footage of the couple and then Michelle's drawing along with several others."

"Like a photo lineup. Great idea."

The younger sister, Annie, came across the store to greet them. "Did you find anything on the security tapes that'll help you with this case?"

"Yes," Rachel said.

The owner breathed a deep sigh. "I'm so glad because I couldn't give the sketch artist who came yesterday afternoon much to go on." Annie swept around. "Barbara, the Texas Ranger and the sheriff are back," she called out. "She's in the back, checking inventory."

The older sister, whose hair was a mixture of black and gray hair, emerged from the rear of the store. "Annie and I were hoping you would come back. I remembered something about the woman. She was chewing gum when she came in here but threw it away almost immediately."

It was a long shot, but Rachel still asked, "Have you emptied the trashcan she used?"

"Yes, every weekend we clean our place thoroughly." Barbara chuckled. "I knew you would ask, and I even checked to see if the garbage bin had been picked up. Wednesday is when they come. It has already been emptied. They usually come first thing in the morning."

If only they had known about that yesterday. If they had found the gum, they could have gotten DNA from it. "What company do you use?"

"Reuter's Trash Pickup. They're used by everyone in the shopping center. I have their number in my office."

"Do you bag your trash up?" Dallas asked.

Both sisters nodded.

"Great. Could you go get the phone number for me?" While Barbara scurried to the office, Dallas slid the six drawings out of a folder and laid them on a nearby table. "Do you see anyone here who was in your store last Friday?"

Annie studied each one, quickly dismissing the two pictures from her and Barbara. She lingered over the drawing Michelle made after her nightmare. But she moved on and finally tapped the last one—the one Michelle had drawn the previous day. "It's the blond hair. Curls everywhere. The sunglasses are large ones. They capture your attention."

"I wonder what she looks like without the big hair and sunglasses." Rachel watched as Annie again studied the last drawing, then went back to Michelle's sketch from that morning. There were similarities, but the sunglasses camouflaged part of the face so it was hard to say definitely it was the same woman.

"Maybe this one." Annie pointed to the most recent drawing. "But I'm not sure."

"Sure about what?" Barbara asked as she joined them and gave Dallas a slip of paper.

"I'm torn between two pictures," Annie answered.

Rachel asked the elder sister the same questions about the illustrations on the table. "What I saw is this lady." She picked up Michelle's first drawing with the sunglasses.

Dallas opened the laptop and ran the security tape with the woman on it. "You mean this lady?"

"Yes, that's her," Barbara said while Annie hesitated, then slowly nodded. "But the other could be her, too."

"She found the bracelet?" Annie asked.

"Yes." Rachel walked to the basket of skeins on the

floor. "The video showed the bracelet was over here in the basket."

"I talked to my sister last night," Dallas said. "Lenora remembered going through that basket looking at the various colors. But when Brady started crying, she got distracted and didn't realize the bracelet came off while she'd been searching through the yarn."

"Lenora's your sister?" Annie's eyes widened. "I didn't realize that. Has she seen the sketches?"

Dallas took a deep breath. "When we return to Cimarron Trail, we'll show her the drawings and see if she recognizes the lady. Had that woman ever been in your shop before?"

"No, not that I remember, but I'm not good with faces. You're better at stuff like that than me." Annie turned to her sister.

Barbara shook her head. "And I didn't see enough of the man with her to say anything about him." Her forehead furrowed. "I'm so sorry for what's happening to your sister. She's a special customer to us. I remember when I taught her to knit while she was pregnant with Brady. She wanted to make him a baby blanket."

Rachel recalled a pale blue one in the living room. Lenora had been clutching it yesterday while talking to them. "If y'all think of anything else that might help, please don't hesitate to contact either one of us."

Dallas shook hands with both ladies. "Thank you for your help."

Annie stared at the photo she recognized. "We wish we could do more, but we'll keep an eye out if that woman ever returns."

"If that happens, don't say anything to her. Just call

us." Rachel gathered the pictures and put them back in the folder.

When she exited the shop, she paused on the sidewalk and scanned the parking lot. Her eyes latched onto the billboard in a field nearby. "Was the camera successfully installed?"

"Yes, I got a text. Done in the middle of the night."

"Good. Not an easy place to tamper with it."

"The footage is being monitored by the Texas Ranger headquarters. Someone will contact me if they see anything unusual on the surveillance camera."

Rachel crossed the parking lot. "One store down, two to go. Maybe we should also canvass all the places in this shopping center."

"And we still have to visit the employees of the other two places Lenora visited." Dallas opened the drugstore door and waited for her to enter first. "I wish we had two sets of the drawings. It would make this go faster."

"When we go back to Cimarron Trail we can make copies at my station. I'm going to have a couple of deputies canvass Lenora's neighborhood again with both versions of Michelle's drawings. I'm also sending Deputy Jones back to Houston Fowler's ranch and see if any of his employees saw the woman or remembered anything since Monday."

She and Dallas entered the drugstore and approached the manager in his office first to let him know what they were doing. When they showed him Michelle's two pictures, he said, "I haven't seen anyone like that in here, but then I'm often in the back of the store. Maybe one of my employees can help."

They talked to the rest of the employees in the store

and came up empty-handed. Next, they headed for Baby and Things next door. When Rachel didn't see the owner, she walked to Jan Thomas at the back counter and asked, "Is Steve Tucker here?"

"No, he'll be gone all day. Can I help you? Is this about the kidnapping?"

Dallas stood behind Rachel. "We have two drawings to show you." He placed them on the counter. "Have you seen these ladies before?"

Jan tapped the illustration of the woman wearing sunglasses. "I've seen her somewhere, not necessarily here. She looks familiar. It was a while back. Was she involved in the kidnapping?"

"She's a person of interest in the case. If you remember anything about her or where you saw her, please contact us." Rachel gave Jan another one of her business cards.

"I will."

As Dallas and Rachel walked away from the counter, she slanted a look at Dallas, who was deep in thought. "What are you thinking?"

"Something is off." He scrubbed his hand across his nape.

"Why do you say that?"

"She blinked rapidly when she saw the first drawing, then she quickly went to the second one."

"The two pictures are similar. I agree with Annie that the sunglasses draw a person to that picture over the other one."

"Just a gut feeling that something is off. Nothing I can put my finger on."

Rachel hoped he was right, but she hadn't seen anything when talking to Jan. "Or wishful thinking?"

"Maybe, but I'm going to have my office look into Jan Thomas. Let's show these to the other employees."

After they left Baby and Things, it took forty-five minutes to search the other places of business in the shopping center. They ended back at Dallas's car with one last location to visit—an accounting office specializing in tax preparation.

Dallas pulled on the glass front door. It didn't budge. "No one is here."

"It's lunchtime. Maybe they left while we were inside one of the stores." Standing at the large window, Rachel looked inside. "I can't make much out. This glass is meant to make it difficult to see into the office. But there's a desk and chair outside a door that leads to the back."

"I'll have headquarters run down any information on Kendall Accounting, Inc."

While he unlocked his car, Rachel walked around to the passenger side and climbed in. "Let's go talk to Lenora, then get these drawings copied. We can split up and visit the employees who worked Friday separately, since the addresses are scattered all over the place. That way we'll cover more ground."

"Sounds like a good plan." Dallas pulled onto the street that led to the two-lane highway to Cimarron Trail.

Rachel withdrew her cell phone. "I'm calling the ranch to see how our daughters are doing." It rang five times before her dad answered. "How are things going, Dad?"

Her father laughed. "I should be jealous. Katie has taken to Michelle so much she's been ignoring Mom and me. In the barn Katie and Michelle held hands as they walked around checking on the animals. Even when Katie stumbled and fell down, she didn't cry. Michelle scooped her up so fast into her arms and twirled her around that any tears were forgotten as Katie giggled. Tell Dallas he has a very special daughter."

"I will. So, everything is quiet?"

"Yes, or I would have called. We're planning to take Katie riding this afternoon after lunch. But only in the paddock near the barn. I'll be leading the horse while Michelle walks next to Katie."

"Don't have too much fun without me. We're going to see Lenora, then to the sheriff's station. We have more people to track down this afternoon. Give Katie a kiss and hug for me."

"Will do. Any progress?"

Rachel told him about the two sisters identifying one of Michelle's drawings of the woman. "After our visit to Lenora's, we'll be releasing the picture of the lady in both versions. Hopefully someone can tell us who she is and where to find her."

When she disconnected the call, Dallas asked, "How are they doing?"

"Fine. Katie loves being with Michelle."

As they neared Cimarron Lake outside of town, Dallas scanned the stretch of blue water to his left. "We don't live far from here. Michelle and I like to go fishing in a rowboat I have."

"How nice. Do you catch anything?"

"Sometimes, but that isn't why we go fishing. This is the time we share our days with each other."

Rachel twisted toward Dallas. "You tell her about your cases?"

"Not the bad parts. Our chats force me to look at

my day in a good light. When we return to shore, I don't feel as jaded as I did when I started."

Out the corner of her eye, Rachel glimpsed a small moving truck pull into the other lane to pass them. "Looks like the driver is in a hurry."

When the white rental truck was side-by-side with Dallas's SUV, the passenger's darkened window rolled down and a man in a ski mask pointed a rifle at them.

"Gun!" Rachel shouted.

Dallas floored his gas pedal, surging forward. A blast sounded and a shot hit the back window.

Rachel got her weapon and cell phone out. She called the station as the truck pursued them.

"We're under attack by a white rental truck on the highway from San Antonio!"

Suddenly the larger vehicle rammed into the left back side, knocking her phone out of her hand and tossing her against her door. Then it hit them again, shoving the SUV off the road to plunge down a small incline, bouncing over rough terrain and landing in the lake.

# SEVEN

As his car hit the water, Dallas let go of the steering wheel and looked at Rachel. Surprise overtook her expression. The front end of his SUV began to sink—fast. They had less than a minute before they would be trapped underwater.

He unsnapped his seat belt, then released Rachel's. "Roll down your window. We've got to get out."

As he pushed the button to lower his window, he looked at her doing the same. Their windows were halfway down when the power shut off.

With seconds ticking away, Dallas grasped his gun and used it as a hammer to knock out the rest of the glass. Rachel did the same.

As water filled the car, Dallas held his breath and wiggled through the window at the same time Rachel freed herself from the SUV. He popped his head above the water. A shot rang out, a bullet slicing through the water inches from his head. While he ducked under again, he heard another gun going off several times, closer to him. Was that Rachel? He swam toward where Rachel would likely be. He hoped she was all right. The murky lake hindered his ability to see much.

As he made his way to Rachel, every muscle tensed with the expectation of being hit any second. His lungs burned from lack of oxygen. He couldn't stay down underwater too much longer, but he had no idea where the shooter was or if he was still there. Rachel had called for backup before the truck hit them. When would they be here? They were ten minutes from town.

He could no longer hold his breath. He surfaced about ten yards from where they'd gone into the lake. He scanned the shoreline as the sound of sirens echoed through his water-clogged ears. No white truck was in sight, but a red car parked on the shoulder of the road while another pulled up behind it.

Seconds later, Rachel popped up about five feet away. "You didn't get hit, did you?"

"No."

"The shooter was dressed in black with a ski mask on. I shot at him and ducked down real fast. I think I hit him, but I'm not sure."

In the distance, a police vehicle with flashing red lights barreled down the highway from town. "Let's get to shore. The cavalry is arriving."

As he swam to the edge of the lake, another police cruiser joined the first one and another couple of cars had stopped on the shoulder. The two men first on the scene came down the incline and helped them from the lake.

"Thank you. Did you see a white truck?" Rachel asked the guys, dressed in jeans, short-sleeved shirts and cowboy hats, who had stopped to help.

The taller one said, "Yep, heading that way." He pointed back the way they had come.

"I saw a man in black at the edge of the road with

a gun. His partner turned around and picked him up. The guy in black limped to the truck."

"Did you see what the driver looked like?" Dallas climbed up the incline as the first deputy sheriff's car arrived.

"The windows on the truck were too dark to see inside, even when he drove right past me as I was slowing down."

Dallas glanced at his watch. It seemed like an eternity ago, but in actuality, it had been only six minutes since they'd gone off the highway. Bruised and battered, he hurried as fast as he could toward Deputy Jones while Rachel questioned both of the men who helped them out of the water.

"A person in a medium-sized, white delivery truck fired on us and ran us off the road," Dallas told Jones. "It's heading back toward San Antonio. No more than five minutes ago. You and I are going after the two assailants. Rachel and the other deputy can deal with this scene."

Jones nodded. "I'll notify Deputy Ellis. He's right behind me. I was on this road when the call came in."

Dallas hopped into the front passenger seat of the deputy's car as Jones called Ellis about what they were doing. As soon as Dallas shut the door, the deputy sped away from the scene.

After Dallas recounted the events again, Jones called for more backup. "You two must be getting close. Someone is getting very nervous."

"That's what I've been thinking." It had to do with the Chesterfield Shopping Center.

Dallas's gaze swept the expanse in front of the windshield. He didn't want to be surprised again. He'd seen the white truck earlier pull onto the highway from a country road. Its appearance hadn't been anything unusual, nor had its gradual progress to close the gap between it and his SUV.

He sat forward when he glimpsed something white in a copse of trees on the side of the highway. "Slow down." He pointed left. "That might be it. It's not too far from where the truck started following us." Closer to the grove, he tensed. "That's it."

Deputy Jones pulled over and parked on the shoulder, the group of trees only yards away from them. "I doubt they're in the truck."

"Me, too. But let's hope there are clues to who was driving it." Dallas climbed out of the cruiser, drew his gun and crept forward. The assailants might not be in the vehicle, but they could be hiding in the trees.

As Dallas reached the truck, his heartbeat thumped even faster against his chest. "I'll take the driver's side."

Deputy Jones moved toward the right. "The door is open over here."

As Dallas approached the white vehicle, he put on evidence collection gloves, then grasped the handle.

"There's blood over here," Jones called out.

Dallas opened the door and hoisted himself onto the running board. There was blood pooled on the passenger's side floor pad. Rachel's shot had, indeed, hit one of the attackers "I'm calling this in, then we need to follow the blood trail. Check the back of the truck."

Dallas took a few photos of the inside of the truck, then called Rachel, hoping her cell phone was waterproof like his.

"Are you all right, Dallas?"

"Yes. I'm calling with good news. I found the truck and one of the assailants is definitely injured. We're in a grove of trees on the left side of the road ten miles away. I need this truck gone over thoroughly. We're following the blood trail."

"I'll have Deputy Owens come out to the truck. I'm still interviewing the people who stopped and processing this area. Stay safe."

Her last words warmed him as he ended the call. He felt as though they'd worked together for longer than just two days. He hopped down from the running board and headed to the rear of the truck.

Deputy Jones finished his preliminary search of the back. "There's nothing here."

"Deputy Owens is coming to secure this site. I'm going to follow their escape path. When he shows up, come join me."

Dallas found the red splotches on the ground and tracked them, scanning the terrain around as he traced their escape. Deeper into the grove of trees the undergrowth thickened. The wounded guy had lost a lot of blood. He definitely needed medical attention. This might be the break in the case they needed.

Another hundred yards away Dallas sighted a black lump on the ground up ahead. Gun in hand, he rushed forward. When he reached the downed man, he felt for a pulse. Nothing. He rolled him over, face up. Rachel's shot hadn't killed him. A slit to the throat had.

In her office at the sheriff's station, Rachel reviewed the limited evidence surrounding the attempt to kill her yesterday and what little they had discovered this morning on the highway at the lake. Once they identified the dead man in the grove of trees, she hoped more information would be revealed about the shooter. He had no ID on him. Dallas was running his prints right now. They needed a break.

If she hadn't ached before, she did now. Two wrecks in two days. Her body was protesting the abuse with stiffness throughout her body and many of her muscles hurt. Pain radiated down her neck and through her shoulders.

She leaned forward and, with her elbows resting on her desk, cradled her pounding head in her cupped hands. She and Dallas still needed to go see Lenora and the rest of the employees who had been working Friday at the shopping center. Michelle was redoing her two drawings since the old ones had been ruined when the SUV went into the lake. Dallas had snapped photos of the illustrations on his waterproof cell phone, though, so they could show Lenora those.

Her deputies had interviewed the people who had attended the committee meeting with Lenora and nothing panned out. She hadn't thought it would, but the people who knew that Lenora would be at that meeting needed to be addressed, as did Mary Jane Martin, who hadn't shown up at Lenora's house with the papers.

When a light rap on the door sounded, she raised her head as Dallas came into her office. "Did you get a match on the prints?"

"Nothing so far."

Her shoulders sagged. She shoved her chair back and stood. "Let's go see Lenora, then get the new drawings from Michelle. I want to spread them far and wide."

"Rob brought me Michelle's sketches so we won't have to go pick them up."

"Oh, good. Although I'd love to see Katie, this will give us more time to investigate."

"I've put a rush on the shooter's autopsy. His partner must have killed him rather than leave him behind alive. He was a big guy. From the footprints found at the scene, the other person was supporting him the further away from the ditched vehicle they went. I guess he got tired of carrying the guy."

"Every man for himself. Doesn't surprise me. We'll need to see if any of the footprints from the tree grove match the ones from the dirt road we have already." Rachel set her cowboy hat on her head and left her office.

"From the other footprint, it was most likely a man—certainly not the woman at my sister's house unless her feet have grown four sizes."

"I'll have Deputy Jones check to see if the male footprint from the dirt road matches either of the ones from the recent crime scene."

"I think the dead guy was the female's partner. The footprint in the grove was a boot like the one I saw on the dirt road."

"So, our lady kidnapper is still out there. If we find her, we could find Brady." The idea they might be close to solving the case lifted her spirits and helped her to ignore the body aches. "Good thing my sheriff's vehicle was here at the station. Let's try not to trash this car, too."

Chuckling, Dallas winked. "I'll do my best."

"I'd hate to hear what Marvin would say if this car

ends up wrecked, too. He loves to tell everyone what a bad job I'm doing."

"The people know what type of person he is. You were voted in. Not him. He's quick to criticize but never has any plans to fix a problem."

She slid behind the steering wheel of her cruiser and started the engine. "Wait until he finds out I'm taking this car home with me until I replace my own."

"When we solve this case, he'll have to shut up."

"I'm not sure he's capable of doing that." After pulling out of the parking lot, Rachel drove in the direction of Lenora's house. "How are your sister and Paul doing?"

"I talked to Mom a little while ago. They're barely holding themselves together. Every time the phone rings, they hope it's the kidnapper demanding a ransom. Deputy Carson has been screening the calls, and if it's someone they know, Mom talks to them. If anyone can handle it, it's my mother. She's a remarkable woman."

Rachel's late husband rarely wanted to go with her to visit her parents. She'd often gone alone. Justin hadn't even seen his own parents much, even though they lived in Austin. Listening to how Dallas felt about his family only reinforced the type of man he was—caring and loving. She hadn't seen that red flag with Justin until after they were married. She'd been young and madly in love. She wouldn't let that happen to her again. Ever.

Rachel exited her cruiser at the same time as Dallas, and they walked up to his sister's house.

Deputy Carson answered the door. "I heard what happened this morning. I'm glad y'all aren't hurt."

"Do Lenora and Paul know about the ambush?" Dallas asked.

"Your mom does, but I don't think she said anything to them."

"Good. I'd rather they not hear. Lenora and Paul have enough to deal with right now. I'll let my mother know the details, and she can decide when to tell them."

"They're in the kitchen." Deputy Carson shut the front door as they all stepped inside.

Rachel followed Dallas into the kitchen. His expression suddenly turned solemn as he approached the table where his family sat, staring at the half-eaten sandwiches in front of them.

Dottie quickly stood and hugged Dallas. "How's Michelle?" She kissed his cheek and whispered, "And you and Rachel?"

"Fine, Mom." He glanced to Lenora and Paul. "We have some clues to investigate after visiting the Chesterfield Shopping Center yesterday and this morning."

Lenora looked up, a ray of hope in her eyes. "What clues?"

Rachel sat diagonal to Dallas. "Michelle remembered more about the woman who kidnapped Brady. I have three drawings. One with her sunglasses on and two with them off. Because the suspect had dark eyebrows, Michelle did one drawing with the curly blond hair and another with dark. We don't know if the suspect wore a wig, bleached her hair or normally was brown headed."

Dallas slid the three drawings from a folder and put them side-by-side. "Do you recall ever seeing someone like her anywhere?"

Lenora looked at the first illustration, then focused on the next one, then on the last drawing. When she raised her head and looked at Dallas, hope flashed again into her expression. "Yes." She tapped the illustration with no sunglasses and blond hair. "First at Baby and Things, then she came into the Knit n' Pearl a few minutes before I left, but by then she had on sunglasses."

"Was she in Baby and Things before you?" Rachel asked.

"Yes."

"What was she doing? Was there a man with her?" Dallas stacked the drawings and slipped them into the folder.

Lenora cocked her head to the side and stared up at the wall behind Rachel. Then she looked her square in the eye and said, "She was stocking the shelves. She must have been a worker at the store, or at least, that's what I thought at the time."

Rachel exchanged a look with Dallas. Surprise flashed across his face.

"That lady is one of the kidnappers?" Paul slipped his arm along Lenora's shoulders.

"Yes, we think so. We'll be putting her picture out to the press. I'm hoping someone will come forward with information about who she is and where she lives." Rachel rose. "If you remember anything about that Friday and about the man who was with her in Knit n' Pearl, please let us know."

Dallas pushed to his feet. "I'm only a phone call away if you need me. This is a solid lead, Lenora. I'm doing everything I can to bring Brady back to y'all."

Lenora's eyes teared. "I've been praying. God's protecting Brady." She touched her chest. "I know it in here." She placed her splayed hand over her heart.

Dallas gave his sister a hug.

As they made their way to the front door, Dallas's mother followed them. "Son, please take care of yourself. I heard one of your attackers today was killed by his partner."

He stopped. "Where did you hear that?"

"I overheard Deputy Carson talking to someone. I know I shouldn't eavesdrop, but when it comes to my family, I don't want to be kept in the dark. Please, Dallas."

Dallas hugged his mother, then stepped out of the house.

As Rachel and Dallas headed for the cruiser, she said, "We'll stop by the station and give Deputy Jones these drawings to distribute to the local law enforcement agencies and the media, then we need to pay the other employees at Baby and Things a visit."

"We may also have to have another conversation with the owner."

"Sounds good to me. I can talk with Jan Thomas again." Rachel backed out of the driveway. "I'm glad Lenora seems better today."

"Her faith is strong. She was the one, when I moved here, who persuaded me to come to church and re-acquaint myself with the Lord. After Patricia left, I was angry at God. At first I wouldn't go, but then Michelle started attending with Lenora and Mom. When Michelle was the narrator of the children's Christmas play at church, I had to go. I wasn't going to let my daughter down and not see her perform. There are times my job does get in the way, but I didn't have that excuse then."

"How do you reconcile all the evil acts we're exposed to with the idea God is in control? Why would He let something like this happen?"

"This is a fallen world, and we have free will. God wants us to come to Him because we choose to and believe in Him. Challenges and problems make us stronger. We learn to appreciate the good times."

Rachel sighed. "My parents have been taking Katie to church on Sunday since I moved back here. To be honest, I always manage to be busy. I have so much anger toward Justin. He betrayed me, betrayed our marriage."

"We go to the same church as your parents. I hope you'll come with us next time. Our pastor has a gift. I always feel uplifted by the time I leave, and there have been times I didn't think that was possible, especially with the crimes I've worked in San Antonio."

"Have you forgiven your ex-wife?" Rachel asked as she parked in front of the sheriff's station.

"Yes, but that doesn't mean I'm not cautious. I've doubted my ability to read people. I'd always thought I was good at it."

Rachel twisted to face Dallas. "Me, too. I couldn't understand how I could have read someone so wrong. How did I miss the signs of Justin having an affair or the fact he really didn't want a child? Every time I think of what he did to me, I get angry again. Like you, I don't want to go through that again."

"Being able to forgive Patricia has helped me. I found that the anger ate into me and that invaded all parts of my life, even my relationship with Michelle.

That first year we fought all the time." Dallas grabbed the folder with the drawings and pushed the passenger door open. "I'll have a deputy make copies and spread these pictures to law enforcement agencies and the media."

Rachel leaned back in the car and closed her eyes, relishing the first couple of minutes she'd had alone since the attempt on their lives. Three days ago, her life had been routine and calm in spite of Marvin's caustic criticism of her abilities. Coming home to Cimarron Trail had been a good decision for her. She'd missed her family being so close by. Today's shooting only reinforced that she was a target and needed to keep vigilant at all times. She'd grown up here and would never have imagined that a baby would be kidnapped by a stranger. But her small town was becoming more of a suburb of San Antonio. Life in Cimarron Trail was changing.

Challenges and problems make us stronger. Sometimes, however, she would rather not have to deal with problems. Over the past couple of years, it felt like that was all she'd done. And she'd turned away from the Lord. Maybe she should seek His help, because what she was doing was obviously not working.

Dallas left the station and walked back toward the car. He was full of self-assurance, and yet he'd dealt with a problem similar to hers—a failed marriage that had left them both questioning their judgment. She admired his perseverance.

He climbed into the passenger seat. "Deputy Jones is making sure the pictures go out to the press ASAP." He laid the copies in his lap. "I'm hoping one of the

Friday workers at Baby and Things will be able to tell us who this woman is."

"According to Lenora, she is one of the workers, and yet Jan hadn't been able to ID her when we showed it to her earlier today."

"Or maybe the lady was only pretending to be a worker."

"You think the woman wasn't actually working at the store?"

"It's a possibility. She was at the front. The others were at the rear or the other side. When I go into a situation, I try to look at it from all angles. That way, I'm not as surprised if something happens because I've considered all sides."

"We only have two more people to talk to about working Friday. Carrie Zoeller and Lynn Davis. We know that Betty, Jan and Steve, who also worked that day, aren't even similar to our suspect, so if it's someone at Baby and Things, it would be either Carrie or Lynn. The nearest one is Lynn." Rachel headed for her apartment.

As she passed the lake where Dallas's SUV had been forced off the road, her grip on the steering wheel grew tighter and her attention kept shifting between what was in front of and what was behind her.

"My car has been pulled out of the lake and towed away. A new vehicle for me is being delivered later today at your family ranch, although I think we should stick together."

Together. Back in Austin she'd had a partner, but she'd never felt this kind of connection with him. "After what's happened the past few days, I have to agree. I hope our shooter today will be identifiable. We need a lead." As she drove by the grove, she could see that the crime scene had been processed, but there was nothing among the trees to indicate a man had been murdered. "Whoever is behind the kidnapping doesn't want to leave any loose ends. The guy who was killed was the man I caught at the side of your sister's house."

"So the driver killed the male kidnapper rather than leave him alive to talk. That's half the team who attacked Michelle."

Rachel tossed Dallas a quick look. "She seems to be better today. More relaxed at the ranch."

"Katie has something to do with that."

Dallas smiled.

Ten minutes later Rachel pulled into the parking lot at the apartment building where Lynn Davis lived. There were only a few cars around. "It looks like most everyone is at work."

Dallas knocked on the door of apartment 2E on the second floor. He waited a minute and rapped his knuckles against the door again.

"Hold your horses. I'm coming," a female voice shouted from inside.

Dallas held up his badge so Lynn could see his identification.

The lock clicked, and the door swung open. "Has something happened in this building? The cops are here at least once a week." Her curly hair tousled, the middle-aged blonde, dressed in a robe, blocked their entry into the apartment. "I need to get ready to go to work. I've seen and heard nothing."

Rachel stared at the woman's hair, almost the same as their suspect, and put her hand on the butt of her holstered gun. "You're going to Baby and Things?"

"No, that's only my weekend job. I work at Lone Star Tavern, not too far from here." Lynn crossed her arms over her chest.

Dallas crowded closer to the woman until she had to step back. "This is about last Friday at Baby and Things."

Lynn switched her attention to him. "Nothing happened there. It was a boring, uneventful day."

Dallas held up Lenora's photo. "Do you remember seeing her on Friday?"

Lynn's eyebrows crunched together. "Not on Friday but she seems familiar. I could have waited on her once before. What's wrong?"

"Her baby was kidnapped." Dallas showed Lynn the drawing of the suspect. "Have you ever seen her in the store?"

Lynn's eyes grew round. "Why?"

"She's a person of interest in the case." Rachel dropped her hand away from her holster. Lynn Davis didn't look anything like the woman in Michelle's drawing, except for the hair.

"What time are you talking about on Friday? I was late for work because my car broke down and I had to have it towed to a garage. I didn't show up until noon."

Although Rachel didn't think she had anything to do with the kidnapping, Lynn's alibi would have to be checked. "Have you seen this lady at any time?"

"Maybe the one as a brunette."

"When? Where?"

Lynn shook her head. "Maybe the store or the tavern. I don't know."

Rachel handed the woman her business card. "If

you remember where or when you saw her, please let me know right away. A child's life is at stake."

"I will."

Dallas touched the brim of his cowboy hat. "Thanks, ma'am. We appreciate it."

When they returned to the cruiser, Rachel glanced up to the window that would be Lynn's apartment. The blonde was watching them. "For just a second I thought we had our suspect, but she looks fifteen or twenty years older."

"Yeah. She is, not to mention her eyes and brows are different."

"And her nose isn't even close."

"Let's go see Carrie Zoeller."

Twenty minutes later, Rachel parked in front of a small, one-story house in a neighborhood not far from the shopping center. A tricycle sat on the porch.

Dallas rang the bell once, then again a minute later. "She must be gone. The carport is empty."

Rachel glanced up and down the street and noticed a car in the driveway of a neighbor's place. "Let's talk to whoever lives next door." Before leaving, she took her business card out of her pocket and scribbled a note on it for Carrie to contact her.

With Dallas next to her, she left the porch and crossed the yard, approaching a teenaged boy washing his white Mustang. "Do you know when Carrie Zoeller will be home?"

The boy looked over his shoulder and shrugged. "She left about an hour ago. Don't know where she went."

"I saw a tricycle out front. Does she have a child?"

"Yep, two boys."

"What are their ages?" Dallas interjected.

"Two and four, I think. Is something wrong? She's a nice lady."

Dallas held up the two drawings of the suspect. "Have you ever seen anyone around here that looks like this?"

The young man shook his head. "No, sir."

Rachel smiled. "Thanks."

As they walked toward the cruiser, her cell phone rang and she noticed the call was from Deputy Jones. "Yes. What's going on?"

"There's been another baby kidnapped, in Guadalupe County. Same MO as ours."

Rachel's heart sank.

# EIGHT

As Rachel drove back to Cimarron Trail from Guadalupe County later that day, Dallas's mind swirled with all the clues and unanswered questions concerning the case. "If there had been any doubt about Lynn, we know for sure she isn't the woman who abducted Brady nor the Rands' five-month-old baby boy, Chris. She couldn't be in two places at one time."

"The kidnappers are bold, snatching their son Chris from his bedroom while he was napping. I wasn't even sure it was part of the baby 'shopping' ring until Mrs. Rand talked about going to Baby and Things two days ago. It's too late to go pay the owner a visit at his store."

"But not his home. I had my office send me his house address. Let's drop by and have a little chat with the man. It's only half an hour away." Dallas plugged where Steve Tucker lived into Rachel's GPS system in the cruiser.

"Why these babies? It's as if they are being selected for a reason. There's nothing random about these kidnappings."

"Like a designer baby ring. They're picking the

children from a list of certain traits. Mr. Rand is a professor at a college and Mrs. Rand is still on maternity leave from her law practice. Paul is an accountant. Lenora has a college degree in biology, and before she had Brady she worked at a scientific laboratory. We need to check on the backgrounds of the parents of the other babies abducted in Texas."

"They're going out looking for certain traits and attributes of a child. That means there's a lot of money changing hands." Rachel shuddered. "The ring must have many people working for it if this is the same one as the other places in Texas. I think we need another press conference tomorrow. If we tell people what's going on, maybe someone will come forward with information that leads to the ringleader's arrest. I'm going to send a deputy to both sets of parents to make sure they haven't crossed paths somewhere else besides Baby and Things."

"It might not be the store but the shopping center. Now that we have video feed from the billboard, we'll need to go through it and follow Mrs. Rand's footsteps there a couple of days ago."

"That would be good to do tonight after we see the owner."

"And eat dinner. We forgot about lunch." Dallas grinned. "And I have the perfect place."

"Oh, where?"

"It's a surprise. I'll drive after we see Steve Tucker."

"Only if you promise me that I'm dressed appropriately for this mysterious eatery."

He chuckled. "Of course. Seeing as we're both dressed in our uniforms." Feeling the urge to make their lives a little bit normal under the circumstances, he decided to take her to his favorite restaurant as… what? Partners? Friends? Or more? In three years, he hadn't been interested in dating, but what he saw in Rachel made him want to rethink his decision to go it alone.

Ten minutes later, Rachel pulled up to the curb in an upper-middle-class subdivision in San Antonio. "Nice place. I didn't realize Mr. Tucker was doing so well."

"Interesting, probably close to five thousand square feet. I've had Taylor at headquarters running some background information on him. We should have it by tomorrow."

As they approached the Tuckers' house, which had lights blazing from it, she paused at the bottom of the porch steps. "Since this isn't my county, you should take the lead. I'll sit back and watch his microexpressions. A baby store would be a good place to search for the perfect matches if you were going shopping for a child."

"May we have a word with you, Mr. Tucker?" Dallas asked when the store owner opened the front door.

Steve Tucker's eyes widened as he looked from Dallas to Rachel. "What's wrong?"

"There's been another kidnapping that has a similar MO to the one in Cimarron Trail."

"What does that have to do with me?"

"Mrs. Rand visited your store two days ago. Your shop is the common denominator with the two abductions. You told us you delete your footage after two days. Since Mrs. Rand was there on Monday afternoon, you should still have it. We need to look at it. Tonight."

Tucker's face blanched. "Sure. Anything to help Mrs. Rand. Let me get my car keys."

"That's all right. We'll drive you." Dallas didn't want any reason to think that the store owner would call someone to get rid of the tapes. Tucker couldn't be ruled out as part of this baby ring.

"Okay. I need to tell my family where I'm going."

As Dallas followed the man to his den, Tucker glanced over his shoulder twice but didn't say anything. He kissed his wife's cheek and said something to her that Dallas couldn't hear. He stepped farther into the room.

Tucker straightened, his shoulders stiff. "Let's go." In the hallway, he turned toward Dallas. "My store had nothing to do with these kidnappings. I started my store to offer lower prices than other places because I wanted to support families with children."

"Something on your security tapes might help us figure out this case. We don't have time to wait until tomorrow morning to see what that is. Two babies' lives are at stake. Two sets of parents are worried about their children. If you aren't involved, you have nothing to be concerned about."

"It was a good thing you came now because the system will automatically tape over the previous recording tomorrow morning when it starts up right before the store opens."

Dallas climbed behind the steering wheel while Rachel sat in the backseat next to Tucker. The trip to the store only took twelve minutes. Dallas hoped this would give them the clue to break the case wide open. He parked in the back of the shop. When he switched off his engine and the headlights went out, the surroundings were pitch black.

Dallas leaned over to retrieve his flashlight from the glove compartment. "You don't have a security light out here?"

"Yes. It comes on automatically when it gets dark. It must have gone out."

Dallas opened the door. He didn't like this. "Y'all wait here. I'll check the store out first. Do you have a security system?"

"Yes. My code is 2975. One of the pads is inside the back door and another at the front entrance."

Dallas strode to the rear of the store, inserted the key and turned the knob. He eased the door open, flipped on the lights and entered the code on the security pad. Then he stepped around a stack of boxes nearby and crept toward Tucker's office where he turned on another switch. Light flooded the room. On the desk sat a computer, and on the counter to the left was a small TV. Everything seemed to be in place, but before bringing Tucker inside, he quickly made a sweep of the whole store.

Maybe the security light had gone out on its own. Maybe not. Dallas quickly returned to the cruiser. Rachel and the store owner walked with him back into the building. Tucker paused by the stack of boxes and frowned.

"What's wrong?" Rachel asked.

"These weren't there when I left. Did you move them?" Tucker looked at Dallas.

"No, I walked around them. Where were they originally?"

The store owner slid the three boxes a foot closer to the door. "I put them right by the back, so when I come inside tomorrow morning, I immediately put them in the trash out back or I'll forget to throw them away."

"Who else uses this door?" Dallas walked to the office.

"Delivery people throughout the day, but my employees come and go using the front entrance. Our space in the rear is limited, and I'd rather my deliveries come through the back so we need to leave some space for them to park." Tucker shrugged and followed. "I guess I forgot to pull the boxes closer to the door when I left. This week hasn't exactly been a normal one ever since you came to visit on Tuesday."

"Let's make this quick. The sheriff and I still have things we need to do."

Tucker crossed to the cabinet below the small TV, opened the two doors, turned on the television and then punched a button on a VCR. Nothing happened. He tried to eject the tape, then looked over his shoulder at Dallas. "The tape should have been in the machine. I took yesterday and today's tape out and put in my older one with Monday and Saturday footage on it so when the VCR started recording tomorrow it would be ready to go. I don't know what happened. I only use two tapes. I've never been robbed. My alarm system has been good in keeping burglars away."

"Let's play the other one." Dallas squatted in front of the cabinet and searched for the second tape while Rachel walked around the office, checking for any place that might conceal a VCR tape.

"I'll take fingerprints off the VCR and TV as well as the front and back doors and the security pads nearby. I'll get my kit." Rachel left.

Tucker shot to his feet and spun around, looking frantically everywhere. "Someone must have been in here. Was the alarm on?"

"Yes. Who knows the code and has a key to the store?"

"Jan Thomas and Betty Biden both have a key. If I can't open Baby and Things for some reason, one of them will. I give them the code, then change it after they've used it."

"So having the key but no code wouldn't allow them to get in without the alarm going off?"

"Right. And I change my code once a week whether I've had one of them open for me or not."

Could one of the ladies have gotten the code without Tucker knowing or was something else going on here? "How long have they worked for you?"

"Betty was one of my first employees fifteen years ago. Jan has been with the store for five years. Neither one would have done this."

"Are they working tomorrow?"

"Yes."

"We'll be here before you open in the morning. Let's walk around and make sure the tape is the only item taken."

As Dallas followed the store owner onto the main floor, Rachel wrapped up taking prints from the front door. She looked at him with a tired expression. He'd been in one wreck, but Rachel had been attacked several times. All he wanted to do was hold her and protect her. If he suggested she back away from the investigation and let him continue, he was sure she would refuse. Short of being in a hospital bed, Rachel would stay on this case until the kidnappers were caught. No matter what.

Rachel sat at a table for two in Cimarron Trail Café across from Dallas. "Something doesn't feel right about Baby and Things," she said. "I feel like when we get near a clue that might break this case open, something odd happens, like the VCR tape has been taken."

"Yeah, and according to Tucker, not by him. So, who?" Dallas ran his hand over his jaw. "We'll need to take every employee's fingerprints tomorrow to be able to rule them out, then we'll see who is left."

"I think it's someone in that store. Mr. Tucker has an old surveillance system, but customers wouldn't know that from looking at his cameras in Baby and Things."

Dallas finished his last sip of coffee. "Taking the prints from the employees and matching them with the ones you took from the equipment, we can rule out the possibility someone came in from the outside and took the tape. Then we really dig into their lives."

"Of course! I should have thought of that. In my defense, I'm a little exhausted after being attacked for the past three days."

He chuckled. "You and me both."

Rachel's cell phone rang. She quickly answered the call from headquarters. "Sheriff Young."

"This is Deputy Jones. There was a match of the boot prints at the crime scene today. The dead man was one of the kidnappers. The same boot print, down to the sole being worn on the inside, was one of them on the dirt road."

"Any results from the dead man's prints?"

"So far not in the system, but we do have a picture of the male kidnapper."

She'd hoped he could be identified by his fingerprints, but they still had their best lead now that they could put the dead man at Lenora Howard's and at the grove near the lake. "I want it released to the media.

Someone might recognize him, which could lead us to the woman kidnapper."

When she ended the call, she couldn't contain the smile that spread across her face as she told Dallas what Deputy Jones had said.

"Now all we need is someone to come forward to ID if not him, then the woman. I'll be praying for that."

"Me, too." When she said it, she realized she meant it. She hadn't prayed in over a year. It was high time she did.

"But identifying the kidnappers is only the beginning. This ring obviously has multiple people involved. We need to get a search warrant for Baby and Things just in case Tucker refuses to let us investigate his store tomorrow. I'll work on the warrant and get it before a judge first thing in the morning. Then we'll return to Baby and Things." Dallas covered her hand with his. "You know, we're a good team, you and I. And I just know that the answer is at that shopping center."

The touch of his palm on her skin warmed her from the inside out. Spending forty-five minutes eating dinner with Dallas in the middle of all the chaos had given her a chance to catch her breath and work her way through the information they had gathered. But mostly she felt valued and knew in the end she was the right person for the job of sheriff, despite Marvin's disparaging remarks since the first kidnapping.

"I've appreciated your help on this case, especially since it's crossed county lines."

Dallas cocked a grin. "I would have helped, even if you hadn't asked me, but don't tell my boss that. Officially I'm on vacation after such a long, intensive case."

"I understand. When someone close to you is attacked, neither one of us is the type to be standing on the sidelines watching others try to figure out what's happening."

His dark brown eyes softened, capturing her full attention. "I feel like I've known you for months rather than days."

She smiled. "We're a lot alike. I had partners in Austin, but you're the first that has made me feel comfortable from the beginning. Although we were partners for years, my first one was male and made it clear from the beginning he didn't want a female partner. After months of getting used to each other, we finally had a good relationship. I often ended up questioning a suspect while he put together the clues to take the case to another level. I learned a lot from him and he from me."

"That's a good partnership—respecting each other and working together rather than against each other."

"I've been in law enforcement for eleven years and still have a lot to learn."

"I'm always learning, and I've been in this field fifteen years."

In that moment, with his hand still cupping hers, a bond between them strengthened. Justin never really had accepted that she wanted to be in law enforcement as a career.

The waitress approached and laid the bill on the table by Dallas, severing their connection.

She reached for the check, but he snatched it up before her. She scowled. "You're helping me on your vacation. The least I can do is pay for dinner."

"Nope. It was my suggestion to come here. The food is great, and the atmosphere is calming in here.

After the day we had, calm is good." Dallas removed money from his wallet and put it on top of the check. "We'd better go. We need to work on the warrant."

"And get some rest, somehow. One of my father's best pieces of advice when I won the election was not to work so hard that I can't be effective. Rest is important in keeping your mind sharp."

"Good advice. I don't always follow it, but I try to."

"The same, but don't tell Dad." Rachel rose and started for the exit.

While she drove to Safe Haven Ranch, she listened to Dallas talk on his cell phone to Texas Ranger Taylor Blackburn at the San Antonio office. Their conversation had to do with the surveillance of Chesterfield Shopping Center from the billboard camera. She hoped there was something that would help them on the footage, and by Dallas's tone of voice, there was.

When he finished, he looked at her, and she caught sight of his grin in the glow of a car's headlights passing them going the opposite way. "A dark compact car came into the parking lot thirty minutes before we arrived at Baby and Things. The person parked at the far end and walked toward the store. He was dressed in black. The one good look from the angle of the camera indicated the guy was wearing a black ski mask. Under the awning the video feed lost sight of the man at the drugstore. There are three shops in a row we can't see the front door. But the guy in the ski mask had to have gone into one of them."

"So, we don't know for sure if he went into a place or even which one? I wish the camera could have picked up the area in front of Baby and Things."

"I do, too, but in order to remain hidden and still

see the whole parking lot and both sides of the shopping center, it had to be mounted where it was. The good news is that the camera caught the license plate number of the car. It's being tracked down. Taylor will let me know when he finds the owner and vehicle."

Rachel turned onto the gravel road leading to her parents' house. "The tire tracks behind your sister's home were from a compact car. It could be the same."

"That was what I was thinking. And remember, a man wearing a ski mask blacked out the lens on the outside surveillance cameras for Baby and Things and the drugstore. What if the guy went into the store and wiped the tape clean after Lenora visited the shop on Friday?"

"But tonight the tape was missing."

"Maybe the person didn't have the time to erase the tape so he just took it. He knows we're closing in on him." Dallas called Tucker to check as Rachel parked in front of the house.

When Dallas disconnected, he opened the passenger door. "Tucker said he changed out the tapes on Saturday night before he left, and on Monday the one he put in the VCR was still there, but he never checked to see if it had been erased."

As Dallas climbed from the cruiser, Rachel did, too, and joined him as they headed to the house. "We must be making them nervous. He didn't want to stick around and erase the tape. Instead he took the whole thing, knowing that would call attention to the store. The ring may be moving on."

"Or they are using another way to target a baby with the attributes they want. I have to admit the baby store is a good way to see a lot of children. I'll call Taylor back and have him check with the other locations where there were kidnappings and see if a baby store could have been involved in those cases."

While Dallas remained on the porch, Rachel went into the house. She needed to hold her daughter. She found her family and Michelle in the den. Michelle was playing with Katie on the floor. When her daughter saw Rachel, Katie pulled herself up and toddled toward her mother with a big smile on her face. Rachel swept her up into her arms. She didn't want to let her daughter go.

"I see Hurricane Katie destroyed your block tower," Rachel said to Michelle. "She loves to do that."

The teen continued to stack blocks on top of one another. "Where's Dad?"

"On the porch talking on his phone."

Michelle hopped to her feet. "I'll be back in a sec," she said.

As Michelle left the room, Katie reached out, opening and closing her hand. "Mimi. Mimi."

"She'll be right back, sweet pea." Rachel carried Katie to the couch and sat next to her mother. Her dad was in the lounge chair across from them. "How did the ride go today?"

Her father smiled. "She's a natural. I see her riding by herself in a few years. Like you, Rachel."

"How's Michelle doing? Has she talked any more about the attack?"

Her mom shook her head. "She's a natural with Katie. Keeping Michelle busy with her has been good for both of them."

Her daughter began wiggling in Rachel's lap. She put her back down on the floor. Katie waddled to the blocks and sent them flying with a giggle. Then she headed out of the den.

Rachel pushed herself to her feet. "She's a girl on a mission." No doubt looking for Michelle.

As Rachel exited the den, she glimpsed Katie disappearing around the corner heading toward the foyer and living room. When Rachel found her in the entry hall, her daughter was turning around in a circle, a frown crinkling her forehead.

"Mimi?"

Before Rachel could respond, Michelle shouted from the porch, "You don't understand. You can't!"

As Rachel snatched Katie up in her arms, Michelle shoved the front door open, stomped across the foyer and took the stairs two at a time.

Katie followed her, her forehead crinkled. She tried to twist from Rachel's arms. "Mimi! Mimi!"

"Let's go see Nana, sweet pea." She held her close as she hurried back to the den. Why was Michelle so angry at Dallas?

Dallas leaned against a post on the porch, darkness blanketing the landscape. The second Michelle had stepped out of the house she'd wanted to know everything going on in the case. He told her they were making progress, but that was all he'd said.

Behind him the front door opened. He looked over his shoulder as Rachel approached him, worry on her face.

She stood next to him. "Are you all right?"

"How much did you hear?"

"Only when she stormed into the house."

"She doesn't want me to work the case anymore."

"What? Why?"

"She wouldn't tell me." He dropped his head and stared at the step below him, kneading the tight muscles in his neck with one hand.

Rachel clasped his free hand. "Wait till she calms down. A lot has happened to her."

"I know. I should be here for her, but we're too close to a breakthrough. I can't stop now."

"Remember she's the one who insisted you look for Brady."

"And if my nephew isn't found, I know my daughter. She'll blame herself." He took Rachel's other hand. It felt so right standing there with her.

Rachel rose up on tiptoes and brushed her mouth against his. "Also remember she's nearly fourteen, and that's not an easy time for a teenage girl."

He slid one arm around her waist and brought her closer, kissing her. "Thanks for being here."

"I could say the same thing." She reached up and cupped the side of his face. "Tell you what. I'll go up and see if Michelle will talk to me. Katie needs to be put to bed. I'm glad I'm here to do it. I'll see if Michelle wants to help me."

He touched her hand on his face, brought it around and kissed the palm. "Thanks."

After Rachel left him alone on the porch, his cell phone rang, and he quickly answered a call from Taylor. "Did you find the car?"

"Sort of. I found the person who owns it. It's Jamie Johnson and he lives at the Fowler Ranch."

"I'll go pay him a visit. Thanks." Dallas glanced at the front door. He'd go see the guy alone and let Rachel be a mother. That was the least he could do for her.

# NINE

After Rachel turned off Katie's overhead light, a soft glow from the nightlight illuminated the room as she and Michelle tiptoed out into the hall. "She's finally asleep. I wasn't sure she would lie down. Thanks for helping me."

Michelle lowered her head. "I'm sorry about earlier downstairs. I hope I didn't scare Katie."

"You didn't. Are you all right now?"

"Yes—no."

Rachel smiled. "Which is it?"

"No." The teen's shoulders hunched forward. "Dad's probably angry with me."

"No, he isn't. Just concerned. So am I. We're getting closer to finding Brady. He thought you would be happy about that."

"I am, but y'all were in a bad wreck today. Someone was shooting at you. I can't lose him, too!"

Rachel's room was across from Katie's. "Come on in here and tell me how you found out about it. We didn't want you to know."

"How much have you kept from me?"

Rachel sat on her bed while Michelle began pacing. "That's the only thing that happened to him."

"But not you. I overheard your mom and dad talking about your near misses."

Rachel patted the mattress next her. "Sit down. I'll tell you what we've been doing these past few days." She recounted everything from her wreck to possibly finding the getaway car in Brady's kidnapping. "If we discover whose car it is, we might have found the kidnapper."

"I shouldn't have yelled, but…" The teen glanced away and rubbed her thumb into her palm as though she were trying to pierce a hole in her hand.

Rachel waited a moment for her to finish her sentence. When she didn't, she asked, "But what?"

Michelle lifted her face and looked at Rachel. When the teen opened her mouth to reply, nothing came out.

Rachel slipped her arm around her shoulders. "You don't have to tell me, but you should tell your dad what's bothering you."

"I can't! I—I don't want to remind him."

"Remind him of what? You can tell me, honey."

Tears pooled in Michelle's eyes. "My mom left my dad because of me."

Rachel's heart cracked at Michelle's pain-filled words. "Why do you say that?"

"I heard her and Dad fighting. She told him she was leaving. She didn't want to be a mother anymore—that there was more to life than that. Dad tried to get her to stay, but she told him that he could have full custody of me. The next thing I heard was the front door slamming shut." Tears flowed down her face, dropping onto her lap.

Rachel's own eyes welled up with tears. She drew

Michelle into her embrace, her heart cracking apart at the sound of the girl's sobbing.

"I can't lose Dad," Michelle mumbled, cradled in the shelter of Rachel's arms.

Katie would never know her father. Even if he had lived, Rachel didn't think he would have been part of Katie's life. The thought broke her heart.

Finally, Michelle pulled back from Rachel and gently swiped her tears away. "Please don't tell Dad."

"I promise I won't, but I do recommend you have a talk with him."

"Oh, Rachel, what if he dies?"

"As you know, my dad was the county sheriff for a long time. I remember when I was a young girl I kept chewing on my clothes. I was ruining shirt after shirt. Mom finally sat me down and asked me what was going on. It had been my way of handling the stress of watching Dad leave each day and go to his job. Not long before that, he'd been in a shootout. He didn't get hurt, but a deputy did. I kept thinking that could be my father."

Michelle's eyes grew round.

"Mom called Dad into the room, and we talked about how I was feeling. He hugged me, then looked me right in the eye and said, 'You can't worry about when you'll die. That's in the Lord's hands. Only He knows the time, and until then, He wants you to enjoy every moment of your life. That's called living to your full potential.' I never forgot those words. My dad was meant to help people and keep them safe. In that moment, I knew I wanted to do the same thing when I grew up." Her father's words had changed her but also had brought her closer to the Lord. She'd lost her trust in God, and the hate and anger toward her husband had filled in the void. That needed to change.

"How can I stop worrying?"

"That's a good question, and I've struggled with that. But I'd forgotten another thing my dad told me. Trust God. If you do, you don't have to worry. I haven't been doing that lately. I've been angry at God. That can take over your life, and you begin to look at everything in a negative light."

"So you think I should talk to Dad?"

"Yes, when you're ready."

Michelle hugged Rachel. "Thanks."

"If you ever need to talk, I'm here for you anytime." Rachel rose. "I'm hoping in the next couple of days we can find your cousin and wrap up the case."

"Me, too. I miss Brady." Michelle rubbed her eyes. "I miss our ranch and my horses."

"You should ride one of my dad's."

"He mentioned that today." Michelle headed for the hallway. "Are you going to bed?"

"No. Your dad and I need to finish some things up first. Good night."

Out in the corridor, Michelle hugged Rachel again, then headed for her bedroom.

Rachel walked toward the den. When she entered the room, she glanced at the table. Empty. Where was Dallas?

She went in search of him. In the kitchen, her father was making a pot of coffee. "I thought you were in bed already."

"Nope. I'm taking the first watch."

"Where's Dallas?"

"He's running down a clue." Her dad searched the cabinet for a mug.

She clenched her hands into fists. "Why didn't he come get me? And what vehicle did he use?"

Slowly her father swung around to face her. "I gave him the keys to the SUV delivered late today for him. He called Deputy Jones to meet him at the Fowler Ranch so he'll have backup."

"Without consulting me!"

"I told him I would tell you. You were busy putting Katie to bed. You haven't gotten much time with her these past few days."

"What clue did he get? At least you can tell me that." Hurt mingled with anger.

"Who the compact car was registered to. It belongs to Jamie Johnson who works and bunks at Fowler Ranch. He hasn't been there very long. He used to work on a ranch in the El Paso area."

She thought of how close the Fowler Ranch was to the residential area where Lenora and Paul lived. Had Johnson been stalking them, looking for the right time to abduct the baby? Then what did the lost bracelet and the Baby and Things store have to do with the case? "I'm in charge of this investigation, and I don't like the fact you two went around me." She strode out of the kitchen.

Her father came after her. "What are you going to do?"

"I'm going to the Fowler Ranch right now."

"What about the warrant for Baby and Things? "

"I'll do the warrant later." She exited the house and marched to her cruiser, furious that not only her father but Dallas was trying to protect her.

What right did they have?

\* \* \*

As Dallas hopped from his new SUV at the Fowler Ranch his cell phone rang, and he quickly answered it. "Did you get his driver's license picture?" he asked Taylor.

"Yes, just sent it to you."

"Thanks. I'll let you know what happens." Dallas noted the text from Taylor had come through and opened it. The face of the dead man in the grove stared back at him. Jamie Johnson was the male kidnapper.

Deputy Jones pulled up behind Dallas's vehicle, parked in front of Houston Fowler's main house, and Dallas headed for the cruiser. "We've gotten a break in the case. Johnson was half of the kidnapping team." Dallas showed the deputy the picture of the dead man's driver's license.

"Yeah, the station has received two calls about him. They recognized his picture that was just released to the press."

"Have you called Rachel?"

"Not yet. I thought the sheriff would be here with you."

"Let Fowler know why we're at his ranch. We need to check the bunkhouse where Johnson stayed as well as the men who worked with him. I'll let Rachel know. She was busy so I left without telling her."

Jones smiled. "I think I've got the easier job."

Dallas was beginning to think the same, especially now that he knew Johnson was definitely one of the kidnappers. But she'd looked exhausted when she went inside to put Katie to bed. Dallas leaned against the back of his SUV and called Rachel's cell phone.

"I started to ignore your call just like you ignored informing me of a break in the case," she answered.

From the sound of steel woven through her words, he was in deep trouble. "Jamie Johnson, who works for Houston Fowler, is the owner of the car we saw on the billboard surveillance camera. I—"

"And you didn't think I should be told that," she interrupted, anger fueling her words now.

"Right after you left the porch, I got a call from my office about the owner of the car. Just now I heard from Taylor and received the driver's license of Jamie Johnson. He's the man who kidnapped Brady. He's the dead guy we found in the grove earlier today."

Rachel sucked in a deep breath. "And the guy who attacked me twice. Don't ever keep me in the dark again, even if you think I need the rest. Let me decide. I'm only five miles away from the ranch."

After three attempts to hurt Rachel in so many days, his first impulse was to say she shouldn't have come by herself. What if there was a fourth attempt? But he remained silent.

"Deputy Jones is talking with Fowler right now." Dallas glanced at the deputy talking to the ranch owner. "And Fowler doesn't look too happy." What if Fowler was the person behind the baby-shopping ring? "See you in a few minutes." He disconnected and marched toward the pair on the porch.

Dallas stuck out his hand. "It's nice to meet you Mr. Fowler. I'm Texas Ranger Dallas Sanders, and I'm working this case with the sheriff's department."

The ranch owner glared at Dallas, but Fowler shook his hand with a tight clasp, as though he were challenging him. "It's nearly eleven o'clock at night. I was on my way to bed. A little heads-up would have been nice. Where's Sheriff Young?"

"She'll be here in a couple of minutes. We'd like to search the bunkhouse. Is Jamie Johnson's car here?"

"How should I know? My foreman runs the ranch. I don't have a lot to do with it. I've already cooperated with the sheriff's office a few days ago. We hardly ever use that back entrance into the ranch."

"Who is your foreman and where does he live so we can talk to him, too? When did Jamie Johnson start working for you?" Dallas asked as he glimpsed Rachel pulling up behind the deputy's cruiser.

"Chuck Stallings. He hires the guys that work for me. You'll have to ask him. My real estate company is where my attention is, not the ranch."

Dallas ground his teeth together. "May we search the bunkhouse? Remember, two babies have been kidnapped recently."

"Fine. I'll call my foreman. He'll meet you there. It's behind the barn. The view is blocked from here." Fowler waved his hand in the general direction then pivoted and stormed into his house, the slamming of the front door reverberating through the night air.

"I see Houston Fowler isn't happy with you," Rachel said as she approached.

Dallas frowned and started for the bunkhouse. "That's too bad."

While her deputy stood back, Rachel followed him, matching his strides. "We'll talk later about what you did to me. Right now, have you thought about who was driving Johnson's car tonight to the shopping center? So far, I haven't discovered a dead man can drive."

"Yes, and I'm having my office look at footage

around the shopping center to see if they can figure out where the car went after it left. Also because Baby and Things is in San Antonio, I'm having Taylor, who has been helping out on this case, get a warrant for the store and meet us there first thing in the morning when it opens."

"Was I going to be included in the search of Baby and Things?"

"Yes, of course." He lowered his voice so Deputy Jones couldn't hear. "But I'm not the one who was punched in the face twice and been in two car wrecks. You needed the rest."

"If the circumstances had been reversed, would you have been okay if I'd done that to you?"

"Okay. You're right. I blew it. But my intentions were genuine."

"I can take care of myself."

"I know." And he did. But that didn't stop him from wanting to protect her. He cared about her. He…no, he wasn't going there. Not yet.

Dallas hung back when an older man came around the barn. Rachel greeted him. As he and Deputy Jones approached them, he realized Rachel was talking with the foreman.

"You didn't see Jamie Johnson after he left early this morning?"

Chuck Stallings nodded.

"Did he drive his car or is it here?"

"He drove his car, and he hasn't come back yet. Has he done something wrong?" The foreman looked right at Dallas.

"This is Texas Ranger Sanders. We found Johnson's dead body earlier today. He was murdered."

"I'm really not surprised. It didn't take much to get him angry. But I'll say he was a good cowhand."

"How long has he worked at this ranch?" Dallas asked.

"He's been here a couple of months. I got a reference from a guy in El Paso I used to know. We worked together on a ranch when we were younger."

Dallas paused a few extra seconds in case Rachel wanted to say anything. When she didn't, he asked, "Which ranch?"

"The Ace in the Hole Ranch. He's the foreman there. Mr. Fowler said you wanted to check the bunkhouse. There are only two other cowhands staying there."

"How many cowhands do you have?"

"Twelve. Only the guys who are single choose to live in the bunkhouse. Most of them have been with us for years."

"Are the other two guys here right now?" Rachel asked.

"One is. The other is out checking the herd. Both of them have been with us for a couple of years. Johnson is the only new cowhand. I can unlock his room. Each one has their own space." The foreman walked toward the bunkhouse with a long porch that ran the length of the front.

Rachel glanced back at Deputy Jones. "I'd like you to interview the cowhand in the bunkhouse right now and come back tomorrow to talk with the other ones about Johnson."

"Yes, ma'am."

After Stallings unlocked a door into a room with a bed, an armoire, a table and chair and a TV on a stand, he stepped back. "I'll be on the front porch if you have any more questions."

Dallas swept his arm wide as he said, "Where do you want to start?"

"I'll take the armoire. It's probably where he hung his clothes since there's no closet." Rachel donned her gloves.

While he searched first the bed and under the mattress, then the drawer in the table, he kept glancing at Rachel. The bruises on her face from this guy they were investigating were changing to bluish purple. He wished he could have caught this guy alive, not only for information on Brady's whereabouts but because of what he'd done to Rachel.

She stooped in front of the bottom two drawers in the armoire and began going through his clothing. "I found something."

When Rachel pulled up to her parents' house, half the night had passed, but it had been a profitable one. She opened the driver's door and reached to take in the piece of evidence she'd found in Johnson's room: a photo of a woman who looked just like Michelle's drawing—the one with dark hair.

Dallas parked behind her and climbed out of her dad's truck. They met on the walk that led to the front porch. She slanted a look at him, seeing the exhaustion in his face. It mirrored how she felt.

As they walked, she grasped his hand. "I'm not mad at you anymore. I'm too happy at the leads we've gotten today. I feel we're getting close to breaking this case wide open." On the porch, she paused and stared at the photo she had of the female kidnapper standing in front of the Lone Star Tavern. "First thing in the morning, we'll pay Lynn Davis a visit. She'll be at Baby and Things tomorrow working. She has a connection through her second job to the kidnapper. This may be where she saw her."

"And didn't mention where she remembered seeing the woman there, most likely."

"Lynn could be hiding something. There's a possibility she's caught up in the ring."

Dallas brought their still-clasped hands up between them as he turned toward her. "I'm sorry. I should have waited for you to go to the Fowler Ranch."

She grinned. "You won't get an argument about that with me."

"Did you put out we're looking for the compact car?"

"Yes, statewide. Hopefully it'll be found with the female kidnapper driving with the man who killed Johnson. But I don't think those three are the only ones involved in this ring, especially if we can connect them to the other abductions in Texas."

"We know that Johnson came from El Paso, where one of the kidnapping clusters was. That's one connection." Dallas's eyes softened as he studied her.

Her heartbeat sped. Even as tired as she was, she would welcome a kiss. He lifted his free hand and cradled her face. The warmth of his palm against her cheek sent a thrill through her. Her eyes slowly closed. Anticipation of what would come flooded her system.

The sudden sound of a lock turning then the front door opening broke them apart. She stepped back.

"Well, it's about time you two got home. I hope you were successful in getting more information about the case." Her dad grinned as his attention shifted between them. He stood to the side as Rachel and Dallas walked into the house.

"We're making progress. Tomorrow will be another long day." Rachel kissed her dad's cheek. "I'm heading to bed. Make sure I'm up by seven."

"Okay. The same with you, Dallas? Just so you know, Rob and I are standing guard tonight. If you're going to think tomorrow, you need rest."

"Thanks, Bill." Dallas followed Rachel up the stairs, catching her in the hallway. "I'm glad we aren't going to sleep angry. Thanks for understanding my moment of insanity."

"Put that way, how could I not forgive you?"

He chuckled. "Good night. On second thought, I want to be at Lynn Davis's at nine tomorrow morning before going to Baby and Things before it opens. I'll have a few Texas Rangers help with the store search."

Rachel entered her bedroom and collapsed, so tired she didn't bother to undress. The last thing she remembered before sleep descended was the look on Dallas's face right before her father had interrupted them. She'd never seen that kind of caring in her late husband's eyes.

Did Dallas really care about her that much?

Driving his vehicle, Dallas pulled up to Lynn Davis's apartment in San Antonio. "There's a chance that Lynn didn't see the female kidnapper at the tavern but somewhere else."

"Or she's a good actress and knows who the woman is—may even be friends with her. Her car is here. That's good news." Rachel took a sip of the coffee she'd brought from home. "Five hours of sleep isn't enough for me."

"Me, either, but we'll have time to sleep after we find Brady and Chris Rand. For one thing, I'll feel a lot better when no one is after Michelle."

"You think she's still in danger even after her drawing has gone statewide?"

"Yes, because she can ID the woman in court when we find her." Dallas and Rachel exited his new SUV. "Taylor has informed the San Antonio police about the case."

"It'll be nice to meet him today. He's done a lot of background work on this case for us."

"Yeah, we've worked together for several years." Dallas took the stairs to the second floor.

Down the hall from Lynn's apartment, an older man passed them in the corridor. Dallas knocked on Lynn's door. After a moment, he pounded louder. Again after a minute, he knocked a third time, then tried the knob. The door opened.

He glanced at Rachel. "I don't have a good feeling about this." After drawing his gun, he eased into the apartment with Rachel doing the same.

Dallas stepped into the kitchen right after the living room while Rachel kept an eye on the short hallway to the right. When he didn't find anyone, he motioned to Rachel to head toward the rest of the apartment while he covered her back. She stiffened in the entrance to the only room except the bathroom across from it.

Rachel, still staring inside, said, "Lynn is dead."

# TEN

All color washed from Steve Tucker's face when Dallas knocked on the front door at Baby and Things with Rachel and the San Antonio police while Texas Ranger Taylor Blackburn planted himself at the back exit in case Tucker made a run for it. His store was caught up in this case. The question was how much did he know about what was going on?

Tucker crossed the main floor and unlocked the door. "I thought you got everything you needed last night. I don't know anything about what's going on. Believe me, I would tell you whatever I knew if I did. This is going to ruin my business."

Dallas entered the shop first, with Rachel checking the parking lot one last time before she came inside, too. When they had parked near where the compact car had been last night, Dallas had found a pool of oil where Johnson's vehicle had been. He'd taken a sample of the residue on the pavement to see if it was the same as was on the dirt road behind Lenora's house.

"I'll let Taylor and the other two Rangers in the back," Rachel said and headed that way.

Dallas handed Tucker the warrant. "We'll be searching the whole place. If you cooperate, this will go much faster and you might be able to open later today."

The store owner's mouth dropped. "What am I supposed to tell customers?"

"I would suggest nothing. Keep your closed sign up."

"I have to tell them something."

"Then tell them you were robbed and the police are here to investigate the crime scene."

Tucker opened and closed his mouth several times, but no words came out. "I've been cooperating. I haven't done anything wrong," he finally said in a gruff whisper.

"And I appreciate your help so far, but something is going on here. We have a tape of a man breaking into your store about a half an hour before we arrived last night. The man is tied to the kidnapping ring and one step ahead of us."

Tucker sucked in a deep breath and held it for half a minute. While he released the air, he lowered his head, squeezing the muscles of his nape. "I didn't realize anyone was taking my tapes and replacing them or erasing them. How could I? Nothing was taken from here."

"We'll try to be in and out as soon as possible. In the meantime, stay out of our way so we can do our jobs."

"What about my employees coming in?"

"Sheriff Young will be interviewing them again. And speaking of your employees, Sheriff Young and I visited Lynn Davis's apartment this morning and found her—" Dallas cleared his throat "—dead." At this time, he didn't want to go into details, but he wanted to see the man's reaction. "She was murdered."

Shock deepened the lines in Tucker's face. "Who? Why?"

"We don't know. Was she supposed to work today?"

"No, only Friday and Saturday this week. Can I tell the others when they show up for work?"

"Yes. When will they be here?"

"In the next fifteen minutes."

Dallas made his way to Rachel and told her when the staff would be there. "Interview each one in the storage room. Taylor and the others will check it out first, then comb through the office."

"What are y'all looking for?" Rachel asked.

"Anything unusual. Either someone is watching this store during working hours, an employee is feeding the kidnappers information about people who come in here or they have cameras for them to view the customers at a distance."

"But if they come in every night and take the tape, they could see it on the footage, so why do anything else?"

"True, but how do they know who the person is unless they have an inside person or a way to record a visual and audio account of what's going on in the store?"

"How about Lynn Davis? Maybe like Johnson, whoever is behind this ring is getting rid of loose ends. But she only worked here part-time. There could be another employee involved."

"That's possible. They seem to know when we're closing in on a person and have gotten rid of them."

Rachel frowned. "Watching us?"

"Probably. They were waiting for us on the road from San Antonio." If they were following them, they were doing a good job. He could usually tell when there was a tail on him.

"It's more than watching us. It's like they know

where we're going before we arrive someplace. Lynn was killed only a couple of hours before we got there."

"There could be a leak."

Rachel closed her eyes for a few seconds. "Someone at the station or your office?"

"I don't want to think that, but we may need to consider it. Up until today Taylor was the only Texas Ranger working on the case besides me who might know what we were planning. I've known him for years and can't believe he would."

Rachel pressed her lips together and looked away. "I can't say that about my deputies. There are a couple who are new to the force this year."

Dallas scanned the store, noting another employee had shown up for work. "Let's discuss it when we're alone. Maybe we'll find something in here that will help us."

Rachel nodded, then walked over to the San Antonio police officer who had Jan and Betty with him. Dallas followed her departure, admiring how well she was holding up under the intense circumstances.

For the next hour, Dallas searched the front right side of the store, checking for anything that possibly could be a hidden camera with a mic. Lynn could have told the kidnapping ring about Friday and Saturday customers, but Mrs. Rand had come in on Monday when Lynn wasn't working. So if there was an informant, she would have worked Monday and Friday. There was something else to consider. Lynn was killed because she knew who the female kidnapper was. Did Lynn try to blackmail her or somehow alert the woman she knew she was involved rather than tell the police?

Dallas moved the stepladder he was using to the next section of the shelving and began inspecting every item and possible place to put a small surveillance camera. He especially looked for the kind of hidden camera devices on the market. Then he spotted a smoke alarm that had a pinhole on the side—which was different from the others in the store. He used the stepladder to check it out and removed it from the wall. Upon inspection, he discovered it wasn't a working smoke alarm but a surveillance camera. It was recording what was taking place in the shop from a good vantage point.

By the time he was done, Dallas had found a couple of other cameras, disguised as a digital clock and a picture frame with a baby photo in it. Now they needed to find out where the signal was going. Who was watching Baby and Things?

Taylor Blackburn, one of the computer experts for the Texas Rangers, joined Dallas. "We're finished in the office and the space in the back. Nothing. The sheriff is wrapping up her interviews. I see you've found some cameras."

"Three. Their placement took in the whole main floor of the store. I've taken latent prints from the devices and sent them to our office. Now you get to do what you're good at. Find where the Wi-Fi signals are going while I have another talk with the store owner."

"I don't know who's going to have more fun. You grilling the man or me tracing where the signal is going."

Dallas laughed. "To each their own." He walked toward the rear to find Steve Tucker. How did the cameras end up in this place without his knowing? Or had he put them there?

Dallas stood in the entrance to the storage room as Rachel was writing something on a pad. Then she looked up. She rose, spoke to the SAPD officer, then approached Dallas.

"I'm finished. How about you? Any success?"

He smiled. "Three hidden cameras. Where's Tucker?"

"Taylor said he was through with the office. Tucker hightailed it out of here, so I would say he was in there."

"Let's talk to him. Did you get anything from the employees?"

"Nothing new."

"How did they take the news about Lynn Davis's death?"

"Surprised and shocked. If one of them was faking, then she's very good at acting."

Dallas gestured for Rachel to go into the store owner's office first, and after he did, he shut the door.

Tucker sat at his desk, talking on the phone. "We'll be open later today. I'm sorry for the inconvenience. I'll offer a twenty percent discount on anything you buy this afternoon." He twisted around in his chair, spied them and said, "See you later," then hung up.

Dallas approached Tucker. "How did these items end up in your store?" He showed the owner the photos he'd taken of the smoke detector, framed picture and digital clock.

Tucker studied each photo on Dallas's cell phone, then shook his head. "I have several smoke detectors throughout the store. The other two, I don't know. I see the clock is on the checkout counter. I thought Jan put it there to keep tabs on the time. I haven't seen the frame. I can't tell where you found it."

"It was on the shelf on the other side of the store from the checkout counter. Each item is really a hidden surveillance camera."

"I didn't put them there!" Tucker's voice rose. "And I resent your implying I did."

"I just want to know how they ended up in here. If you didn't, who did?"

The owner rose and faced Dallas. "It has to have been recently. I've been in my office a lot this past month. I'm working on opening another store on the other side of San Antonio as well as one in Houston. Do you think I would be involved with a baby smuggling ring if I was planning to expand? It could ruin my business."

"Who are you working with about expanding your business?"

"My lawyer, Richard Snapp. Talk to him. He'll tell you. In fact, when I've been away from the store this past month, it's been to see him."

"I'll do that."

Tucker scribbled the lawyer's phone number and address on a piece of paper and handed it to Dallas.

"We're wrapping things up, but Texas Ranger Blackburn may have to stay awhile longer." Dallas told him. "You should be able to reopen by one."

Tucker glared at him. "If my business that I've been growing for the past fifteen years hasn't fallen apart."

Dallas stepped out of Tucker's office. Then, in the hall, Rachel said, "Let's talk with the employees about the three photos of the hidden cameras. Other than that, I'm finished."

"I'll come with you, then we'll pay his lawyer a visit."

While Rachel showed each female employee the photos of the hidden cameras, Dallas assessed their reactions. When they said that they thought Mr. Tucker put them there, it seemed genuine, but Dallas had been lied to many times—and some he'd only discovered with further investigation. The problem was they didn't have that kind of time.

Children's lives were at stake.

Rachel entered Richard Snapp's office with Dallas behind her. She shook hands with Mr. Tucker's lawyer. "I'm glad you could make time for us, Mr. Snapp."

"Anything to help the police. Steve called me very upset about what's going on with his business. I've advised him to cooperate with you in any way. How can I help you?" He gestured toward a sitting area near a large window with a clear view of Hemisphere Tower, which dominated the cityscape of San Antonio.

While Dallas asked the lawyer a few questions about his business relationship with Steve Tucker, Rachel scanned the large office. The walls were laden with pictures of Richard Snapp at various places and with many well-known people, like the governor of Texas, a US senator and a former mayor of San Antonio. The lawyer must be well connected and involved in the community.

When Dallas received a call, he looked at the screen and said, "I need to take this." He left the office.

Rachel took over the questioning. "Where's Mr. Tucker looking to expand? He mentioned Houston and another location in San Antonio."

"I was looking at purchasing a shopping center in San Antonio near Olmos Park and Alamo Heights, and working to have Baby and Things as one of the main stores, but with the problems developing with his store, that might not be possible."

"Do you think he has anything to do with these kidnappings?" She asked it deliberately but acted as though she'd asked something she hadn't intended. She waved her hand in the air. "Never mind. I know you can't answer that question. After all, you're his attorney. Forget it."

Dallas reentered the office, his expression unreadable. "Sorry about that, but the investigation is moving quickly."

"I'm glad to help, but I have a client coming in a few minutes."

"I have one last question. Do you own the Chesterfield Shopping Center?"

"I'm part owner in a lot of shopping centers and Chesterfield is one of them. In fact, it was one of my first commercial properties. I'm one of the partners in Reuter's Real Estate."

"Is that connected to Reuter's Trash Pickup?" Rachel asked. So far, the company manager hadn't returned her call from yesterday, and with all that had been happening, she hadn't had time to follow up. The chances they would know where their last pickup of trash for Knit n' Pearl was located was a long shot, especially after listening to the receptionist at the company talk about their process of dealing with their truckloads as they come in.

"Yes. I have a share of that company. Why are you asking about that business?"

"We needed to check some trash from one of the stores at Chesterfield."

Richard Snapp wrote something on a notepad. "I'll contact the company and make sure they return your call."

"Thank you."

"Is there anything else you need from me?"

"Who rented the space where the accounting business was at Chesterfield?"

"I'll have to look into that. I don't know that information." The lawyer stood and extended his hand. "I'll let you know if I can find out."

Rachel shook his hand, then Dallas did. He took a business card out and laid it on the desk. "Text or call me with the information."

Dallas parked his SUV in the sheriff's-station parking lot next to the building and pried his tight hold off the steering wheel. Tension gripped his body. More questions. Few answers.

Rachel stopped Dallas from getting out of the vehicle with a hand on his arm. "We have a lot to process. I'd rather not do it in my office. We still don't know if there's been a leak or not. Let's eat dinner in the park across from here. It's a nice evening and it won't get dark for a while."

"Sounds good to me. We've been stuck in Baby and Things all morning, then my car and the lawyer's office, not to mention the hours in the deserted accounting office next to Knit n' Pearl."

"I hope the Texas Rangers find something at the accounting office that might lead us to who's behind this ring."

"If anyone can, it'll be Taylor." Dallas took the bag of hamburgers and his drink and exited his vehicle. "He's following the money trail. I've also asked him to get a warrant and look into Steve Tucker's finances. With the hidden cameras in his shop, we shouldn't have any problem doing that."

Rachel crossed the street and sat on a bench that faced the station under a big oak tree. Dallas took the seat next to her and handed her the bag with the hamburgers. Taking it from him, she tilted her head back enough that her Stetson didn't hide her beautiful features, even though they were black and blue from the punches. For a moment, their gazes held as though they were bound together. In the past few days, despite being injured several times, she'd kept going, as determined to bring Brady home as much as he was. He smiled, relishing the soft green of her eyes. The corners of her mouth turned up and a gleam added a sparkle to her expression.

"What are you thinking?" he asked.

"Before you looked at me or now?"

"Now." He wanted to know more than what she was thinking. He was attracted to her, enjoyed her company. But how did she feel?

"It's still hot out here. What made me suggest sitting outside when it's still in the low 90s?" She winked and broke their visual link.

He chuckled. "How about before I looked at you?"

"I don't think Steve Tucker has anything to do with the kidnapping ring."

"Why do you say that?"

"Woman's intuition. He's definitely in the middle of it, but unknowingly. His business is successful. Why risk a chance to expand the business to be tied to a baby-kidnapping ring? If it was me, I wouldn't put my main store in the middle of all that." Rachel took a bite of her hamburger and wiped a napkin across her chin.

"You have a point, but I'm going where the evidence takes me."

"That's all we can do, right? One of the reasons I wanted to talk to you out here rather than in the office was what we talked about earlier. What if someone is feeding information to the ring about what we're doing? How can we flush the person out?"

"Who's working the case at the station?" Dallas asked, then took a long sip of his sweet tea.

"Mostly Deputies Jones, Carson and Owens. A couple of others have helped when needed. The problem is that I don't know my staff as well as my dad does. The only one I'm familiar with over the years is Deputy Jones."

"I know a couple from church and working a few cases with your father. I'm especially acquainted with Jones and Carson."

After eating the rest of her burger, Rachel took a swig of sweet tea. "With only two weeks on the job, not one deputy has given me any reason to doubt his loyalty."

"Then let's go talk to your dad. Taylor is working the accounting office angle, SAPD is working Lynn Davis's murder and your deputies are working the death of Johnson. We need to go back to the ranch, talk with your dad, then sift through all the information from the different sources. Still no word on Johnson's car or the female kidnapper and the man who killed Johnson. I don't think they're running the ring, but one of them might lead us to the person in charge of the statewide ring."

"That person might not even live in the area," Rachel noted.

"I have Texas Rangers standing by ready to investigate any leads, especially in El Paso and Dallas where the ring operated."

"Now we just have to get a name. Let's go talk to Dad." Rachel rose and tossed her trash in a garbage can nearby. She headed across the street and paused at the door into the station. "I'm letting Deputy Jones know where we'll be and I want to check on the latest tips we've received."

When Dallas entered behind Rachel, he glanced over the large open room where a couple of deputies were working. One was on the phone, the other on the computer.

Rachel approached Deputy Owens. "Where's Deputy Jones?"

"He got a call and left. Don't know where."

"I'll be at the Safe Haven Ranch." She started to leave, but stopped and looked at Deputy Ellis, who'd just hung up the phone. "Is something wrong?"

Ellis's face turned red. "My girlfriend called me about a photo that she saw on the internet. She just texted it to me."

Rachel marched over to her young deputy. "What?"

He handed her his phone.

As anger flooded Rachel's face, Dallas bridged the distance between them and glanced over her shoulder at a picture of them eating their dinner in the park. The words, "This is what our sheriff does on the job when a baby is missing." Whoever took it had caught the moment when they'd looked at each other and smiled.

"Marvin is like a gnat pestering me every chance he can get." Rachel pivoted and made her way to the exit.

Dallas followed her from the station. "Next time I see Marvin all I'm going to see is a gnat."

Rachel visualized that and started laughing. "Don't

make me laugh. This is serious. Marvin is a sore loser, and he's making my life more difficult."

"It's because he couldn't believe he could lose to a woman, even with your dad being the previous sheriff. Lenora works with him on a committee at church. She runs the group, but Marvin is always trying to take it over."

"What does she do about him?" Rachel asked as she slid into the passenger side of Dallas's SUV.

"She found confronting him directly didn't work. So, instead, she poured out so much charm that he didn't know how to deal with it."

"I'm gonna try that. Use honey rather than vinegar."

"Exactly." At a stoplight he slanted a look at her. "Speaking of my sister, tomorrow I'd like to stop by her place to fill her and Paul in on what we're doing. I've talked with her on the phone, but I think it'll be good to reassure her in person."

"We could now, if you want."

"No, we should go through everything we have. I'll call Taylor and see where he is on who rented the space for the accounting office. I can't leave it to Snapp to get us the information."

"Are you going to talk to Michelle tonight?"

"I'm gonna try. I hope riding today with your dad has taken her mind off what has happened. She's always been a child who takes the problems of the world on her shoulders. But it got worse after Patricia left."

"The important thing is that you're there for her." Relaxing back against the headrest, Rachel hoped that Michelle would finally tell Dallas about how she blamed herself for her mother leaving them and how scared she was that something would happen to him.

"I heard that your mother made a pot roast tonight. Wish we could have been there for dinner. Michelle even helped her cook."

"Knowing Mom, she has saved us some. We can have a late-night snack."

Total darkness had blanketed the landscape by the time Dallas drove up to the gate to the Safe Haven Ranch. As he turned and headed for the house, he said, "Forget late night. I could have some now. After all, we skipped lunch and a hamburger isn't enough for dinner." He parked out front. Lights from the living room illuminated part of the porch.

"I can't wait to hug and hold Katie," Rachel said as they both climbed from the car.

"I feel the same way about Michelle, especially when we're working this type of case."

She withdrew her key rather than ringing the doorbell and inserted it in the lock. When she entered the house, silence greeted her except for the two loud beeps that sounded when someone opened an outside door even when the alarm wasn't on. "Katie shouldn't be in bed yet. It's too early. They must all be in the den. Dad's truck was outside."

She walked down the hallway that led to the den with Dallas right behind her. When she stepped into the entrance, her dad was lying on the couch while Rob sat stretched out in a lounger. Their eyes were closed. Rachel stiffened.

A chill shivered down her spine. Her father would never be sleeping on the job, especially when family was involved and the alarm was off.

"Dad! Dad!"

# ELEVEN

Katie!

As Dallas bent over her father, Rachel raced through the house, checking everywhere. She passed through the living and dining rooms, but saw nothing out of place.

Until she stepped into the kitchen.

Her mother lay on the floor near the sink with the water running. Michelle was stretched out on the tiles on the other side of the table. For a few seconds, all Rachel could do was stare at Michelle, her arm reached out with her hand touching the leg of the highchair.

Where was Katie?

A cry—as though an animal was wounded—reverberated through the room, sending a shudder down her body.

Dallas burst into the kitchen. "Rachel?"

His hand clasped her shoulder, and she wrapped her arms around him. "Your dad and Rob are alive."

"Katie's gone," she said, trembling.

Dallas spied Michelle on the floor and hurried to her, feeling for a pulse. "Have you looked everywhere?"

"I don't have to. I just know it." As though on automatic, she stooped next to her mother, trying desperately to detach herself from a personal connection to what had happened. "She's breathing."

Dallas stood and pulled out his cell phone "So is Michelle. I'm calling 911 and backup. We need to check the rest of the house."

He was right. But she knew what she would find: nothing. While he made the call, she rushed out of the kitchen and mounted the stairs, praying that she was wrong. *Katie has to be in her bedroom. God, please help me find her.*

When she entered her daughter's room, her gaze riveted to the empty baby bed—the empty room. She didn't need to search the rest of the second floor. This was the only place Katie would be left alone.

Dallas came up behind her, wrapping his arms around her as though letting her know she could lean on him. "I'll finish checking the house. Go sit with your mother and Michelle. I didn't see any physical signs they were knocked out. I didn't smell chloroform or any other kind of gas, so I can only guess how they all ended up passed out."

Knocked out? "Someone gave them a knockout drug?"

"That's a good possibility. The doctor can test them for the substance."

"But who…"

"It must be the kidnapping ring. They now have their third baby. We have to find them soon. They could be gone by tomorrow."

She struggled to keep the hysteria from welling up in her, but thoughts of not ever seeing Katie again overwhelmed her. She turned in his embrace and closed her arms around him, drawing strength from him.

"There's nowhere safe anymore," she murmured against his chest, swallowing the tears demanding release. She had to pull herself together. She wouldn't rest until she found Katie.

"This was a bold move—one meant to throw us off balance. It's not gonna work. I promise you no one will mess with my family or yours without severe consequences. I think we're close. When we find out the information on the accounting firm, it may lead us to the person behind this."

She focused on his words, reassuring yet tough. Leaning back, she looked up into his dark eyes, full of concern. She reached deep down for her professional facade. She wouldn't let them win. "I'll be with Mom and Michelle. Check the rest of the upstairs."

When his arms fell away, she missed his touch. With him, she didn't feel so isolated. She believed what he said. She wouldn't face this alone.

As she left the bedroom, Dallas said, "I'll see you in a few minutes."

She glanced back at him, his gaze soothing as it touched hers. Hurrying down the stairs, she wondered how the kidnapper got into the house. The alarm wasn't set, since they were expecting her home, but the two beeping sounds would have alerted anyone in the house that someone was coming in. And when they all went to the barn earlier, Dad would have set the alarm.

A moan came from the kitchen. Rachel quickened her step. When she entered the room, her mother was trying to raise herself from the floor, but she collapsed back onto the tiles, her eyelids fluttering. Although

Mom had looked right at her, she didn't seem to register that Rachel was there.

She approached her mother and shook her shoulder gently. Her eyes were closed now. "Mom, what happened?"

Suddenly Rachel heard a crash from the den. As she hurried out of the kitchen, she checked Michelle who was still in the same position, and then she left to see what had made that noise. She collided with Dallas.

He steadied her then kept moving, drawing his gun. "I heard something."

She followed right behind him, also removing her gun from its holster. "Me, too."

When Rachel entered the den, her gaze was drawn to her father's favorite place to sit. It was empty. He was collapsed on top of the coffee table. He'd probably tried to get up and couldn't.

Dallas lifted her father and laid him down on the couch. Her dad's eyes popped open, staring right at her. But it was as if he wasn't really seeing her. She'd seen people who had been given pills, like roofies, who were awake but paralyzed, not really aware of what was happening around them. How did this happen to her family?

In the distance, the sound of sirens coming closer filled the air.

Dallas headed out of the room, saying, "I'll let them in. Check everyone and make sure they're still okay. I've seen bad reactions to drugs like this."

After checking her dad's pulse, she moved to Rob. Earlier he'd seemed all right, but now his pulse raced. His lips and fingernails had a bluish tinge. She rushed toward the foyer. The paramedics needed to see to Rob first.

As Rachel hurried out of the house, the first ambulance pulled up. "Rob's in respiratory distress. Dad seems fine."

"Michelle and your mom okay?"

"Don't know. I'm going there now. Get the EMTs to the den, then I'll direct the other ambulance to Mom and Michelle."

When Rachel went into the kitchen, she examined her mother and then Michelle, and still found their pulses okay and they showed no signs of turning blue. She released a long breath. Her heart pounded against her chest and sweat ran down her face. She returned to the front porch as two paramedics exited the second ambulance.

"There are four victims down. Two in the kitchen and two in the den. The other EMTs are in the den. I'll show you to the kitchen."

While the paramedics assessed her mother and Michelle, Rachel stood back, watching and listening to them. When her gaze fell on the empty highchair with crackers still on the tray, tears welled into her eyes, and she turned away, feeling helpless. Mom and Michelle were in good hands. She had to find her daughter.

Rachel left the kitchen. Dallas came toward her, his expression one of determination—and a warning for anyone who got in his way.

"How are Michelle and your mom?"

"The paramedics are checking their vitals. Michelle opened her eyes but didn't say anything. They're going to take them to the regional hospital. How about Dad and Rob?"

"Rob's in bad shape. The paramedic had to put in a breathing tube. Another team of EMTs are transporting him to the emergency room. Your dad is groggy and doesn't know what's going on."

One of the EMTs from the kitchen passed them in the living room, glanced at them and said, "I'm getting a gurney."

As he left, Deputy Jones came into the entry hall with Owens and Carson.

Rachel closed the space between them. "Katie is gone. We've searched the house and she isn't here. My dad's protocol to keep Katie and Michelle safe was to make sure either he or Rob was with them at all times. Even when they all went to the barn, he turned on the alarm, so no one could sneak into the house while they were gone. But the kidnappers must have gotten in somehow, and when they left they locked up, they turned the alarm back on, so my dad wasn't alert something was wrong." She stepped out of the path of the EMT with the gurney who made his way to the kitchen.

"We should go out onto the porch and let them take care of Michelle and your mom," Dallas said.

The three deputies, nearer to the door, exited first.

Dallas clasped Rachel's hand and stopped her, leaning in to whisper, "I want you to go to the hospital. Let me oversee this. One of us should be here."

"But what about Michelle?"

"We don't know who to trust. I'll call Mom, and she'll be at the hospital for Michelle." Dallas looked toward the living room. "I'm not leaving until I know the place has been processed correctly." He released Rachel's hand and walked to the gurney with his daughter on it. After he picked up Michelle's hand, he bent over and said something to her, then helped the EMT take the gurney out the front door. When he passed Rachel, he asked, "Okay?"

She nodded and followed them out onto the porch while another paramedic took an empty gurney into the house for her mother. She joined her three deputies. "Dallas will be in charge. He's staying. I'm going to the hospital. Call for a deputy to meet me there."

"I will." Frowning, Deputy Jones watched Michelle being put into the ambulance. "What happened here?"

"That's what I intend to find out." As her mother was being taken out of the house, Rachel walked beside her to the last ambulance. Right before her mother was loaded into the back of the vehicle, she said to her, "I'll meet you at the hospital. You'll be okay, Mom."

"What's…going on? Where's—" Her mother's words slurred together as though she was drunk.

"That's what I intend to find out."

Rachel quickly ran to her sheriff's car. She wanted to keep the ambulance in her view all the way to the emergency room.

Her cell phone rang. She answered it quickly, thinking it was Dallas, but the second she murmured hello, a mechanical voice said, "You can save your daughter if you mess up this kidnapping case. If you come after me, I will kill her."

Later, after processing the crime scene, Dallas paced outside the room where Michelle and his mother were waiting for test results at the hospital and talked on his cell phone. "Taylor, anything on your end? The kidnappers took Rachel's daughter. We have to find out who is behind this. Now!"

"I'm working on it. The person who rented the accounting firm office space went through several shell companies. They're good at hiding their tracks, but I'm good at hunting them down."

"The quicker the better, man."

"I'll call you the second I do."

Dallas disconnected the call and had started back to Michelle when he spied Rachel coming out of a room. "Rachel."

She stopped "Dallas! How long have you been here?"

"I just got here and checked on Michelle." He closed the space between them. "How are your parents and Rob doing?"

"We're still waiting on test results for Mom and Dad, but I'm pretty sure they were given roofies." She gestured to the room she came from. "I was checking with the doctor about what Rob's test results were."

"How is he?"

"Hanging on. It's been touch and go, but the doctor thinks he's stabilized now. He had Rohypnol in his system but also something else—an opiate. The doctor found a recent mark on his neck. He thinks that's how the drug got into his body. If we hadn't gotten to him when we did, he probably would have died."

Dallas tensed, thinking of the possible lethal effect of mixing the two drugs together. "Are there needle marks on the others?"

"They haven't found any."

He stepped closer and lowered his voice. "Taylor thinks he's close to finding out who rented the office space next to Knit n' Pearl."

Rachel looked up and down the corridor then said, "I got a call from the kidnapper on my way to the hospital. I need your office to trace the call. It's probably a burner phone. I don't think it'll lead anywhere, but we need to try." She withdrew her phone from her pocket and slipped it into his hand, using her body as a shield. "I don't trust my department to do it—not until we find out how the kidnappers seem to know our every move."

"What did he say?"

"I don't know if it was a he. The voice was a mechanical one. I'll be using Dad's cell phone in the meantime. I want you to be the lead on the case, but I'll be working on it behind the scenes."

"I understand. You're too close."

"No, you don't understand. In public I need you to step in and announce because of the conflict of interest with Katie's kidnapping, you have removed me from the investigation and taken over. But I won't let any unknown suspect tell me to sabotage this case. I won't."

He saw a nurse leave a room and walked her way. "Is there a place we can talk privately?" He flashed his Texas Ranger badge.

The older woman nodded. "This way. I don't think anyone is in the chapel right now."

Dallas went in first, checking that the room was empty, then glimpsed Rachel studying the chapel sign next to the door. He took her hand. "It'll be quiet in here." And private. Rachel was barely holding herself together.

He led her to the front near the simple altar with a white cloth draped over it and a cross on the wall behind it. The chapel was quiet and dimly lit. She sat on a padded folding chair, and he took the one next to her. She clasped her hands in her lap and stared at them.

"Rachel, what did the person on the phone say to you?"

For a long moment, she didn't reply, then in a whisper, she said, "'You can save your daughter if you mess up this kidnapping case. If you come after me, I will kill her.' I'll never forget those words, but more importantly the way he said it, as though he meant every word."

"As the news gets out that your daughter has been taken, it'll be understandable that you remove yourself from the case, and therefore can't mess up the evidence. I recommend you back away."

Her head jerked up. "I can't back away. Not now. Do you really think I'll see my daughter again if I follow those directions? The least they would do would be to sell Katie. If I sat around doing nothing, I would never forgive myself."

"And if the person kills her?"

"I'd never forgive myself, but at least there would be a better chance of finding her if I help. No one will be more dedicated. I've already been thinking of clues we need to follow up on." Her eyes glistened with unshed tears. "Do you have any idea what I'm going through? My daughter is in danger because of me."

He grasped her shoulders. "No. She's in danger because there are evil people in this world. And, yes, I know right now you're blaming yourself for everything. I did that on Monday with Michelle. I should have protected her somehow. That's what parents want to do, but we can't always, no matter how much we try."

"She's probably crying right now. She won't understand what's happening to her." Tears coursed down Rachel's face.

He wrapped his arms around her and brought her close against him, sheltering her the best he could. If only they had arrived at the ranch thirty minutes earlier, they might have been able to stop the kidnapping and the terrorizing of their families. He wasn't even sure if *he* should be on the case anymore, because he had a score to settle with the people responsible—for Michelle, Rachel, Katie, Brady and their families.

But there was no way he would walk away from it. Rachel depended on him to find Katie.

As her sobs wet his shirt and tore at his heart, he cradled her closer, wishing he could take her pain away. He closed his eyes and sent up a prayer to God. *Lord, You can do anything. Please show me the people responsible for this crime. Please help me bring Katie, Brady and Chris home safely to their parents. I can't do this without You.*

When Rachel quieted, she leaned back and looked up into his eyes. "Will you and Michelle still stay at the ranch? That will be the only way I can work on the case without anyone knowing but family."

Something bothered him about what had happened this evening. Why had Rob been given an opiate and not the others? "How about Rob?"

Rachel pulled back, squaring her shoulders. "What are you implying?"

"We've been thinking that one of your deputies has been feeding information to the ring. What if it's Rob? You and Bill are close and y'all talk over your cases and what's going on in the county."

"I've known Rob for a long time. He worked with my father for twenty years. Why would he betray our family?" Rachel surged to her feet.

When she started to turn away, Dallas grabbed her hand and stopped her. "I hope I'm wrong, but I wouldn't be doing my job if I didn't look into him as well as your deputies. I have my office checking your staff. I'll be questioning him as well as having your home scanned for bugs."

The tension in Rachel drained from her. "Definitely, but if there are any, they could have been planted this evening. Did you keep an eye on my deputies as they processed the crime scene?"

"Yes. I know how to do my job."

"As I know how to do mine. Did you find anything?"

"So far, nothing. There are fingerprints but most of them can be ruled out right away. Deputy Jones is looking into Rob, but I'm also having Taylor do the same."

Rachel shook her head. "Is this what our job comes down to—question everyone, doubt everyone?"

"I don't doubt you."

"But you question me."

"Only because you can't separate yourself from this case, not with Katie's kidnapping. We have to look at every angle, every possibility."

"I'm going back to see how my parents are doing." She whirled around and marched toward the exit.

He needed to get back to Michelle, too. But not before he begged the Lord for guidance. So much was at stake. He couldn't do this alone.

The next morning, Rachel's eyes popped open, and she shot straight up in bed. Bright sunlight streamed into her room because she'd forgotten to draw the drapes when she got back to the ranch at three in the morning. She glanced at the digital clock on her nightstand. Nine a.m.!

She jumped out of bed and quickly threw on a pair

of jeans and a T-shirt, and slipped into her tennis shoes. At least she would look like she wasn't going to work. Last night she hadn't checked the table in the den. Had the kidnappers taken any paperwork? So much had happened that all she'd concentrated on was making sure her parents and Michelle returned to the ranch with a clean bill of health from the hospital. She was thankful they were okay and home now.

One of her deputies was posted outside on the front porch and another was protecting Rob in the hospital. He still hadn't woken up when she left, but the hospital would call her when he did.

Or rather, they'd let Dallas know. The hardest thing she had to do was look like she wasn't doing any investigating. As the sheriff and mother of a kidnapped child, she couldn't just sit around and do nothing.

The scent of coffee perfumed the air as she descended the stairs to the first floor. She needed to drink some and maybe supercharge her brain. She had to find Katie today. When she entered the kitchen, she came to a halt. With his back to her, Dallas filled his mug, then another one sitting on the counter.

He slowly turned toward her and held out the second mug. "I heard you coming down the stairs."

"I thought it was really quiet upstairs. I'm glad they aren't up just yet. There are a couple of things that need to be followed up on, and we haven't had a chance to go over it with all that's been happening."

"Let's go into the den." Dallas walked a little behind her down the hallway. "I had the house swept for bugs this morning. The house is clean now."

"How many were there?"

"One in the kitchen, one in the living room and one in here."

"Then Rob isn't the leak."

"Are you sure? How did the bugs get in here in the first place? He could have planted them, or if they were trying to get rid of Rob, they replaced him with the bugs. Who else could have done it? Your deputies weren't in here before yesterday and only with me last night." As they stepped into the den, he gestured toward the table where they'd worked. "Everything was moved around, but nothing was taken that I can tell."

"That means they know everything we're looking at. You need to go to the Lone Star Tavern and see if anyone recognizes the female kidnapper. There's a good possibility Lynn Davis was killed because she realized where she saw the kidnapper, especially since we were bugged."

"I agree. Taylor hasn't found any background information or bank records to indicate she was part of the ring. I didn't want to leave until I talked to you. I'd feel better if you or your dad were up. I'm worried about Michelle. We haven't had a chance to really talk. She was still groggy when she went to bed, but she kept telling me to find Katie and Brady. I don't want her to blame herself anymore."

Rachel laid her hand on his wrist. Dallas was torn between doing his job and being a parent. She certainly understood that feeling. She wanted to actively search for Katie, but she needed to appear as though she were taken off the job by the Texas Rangers due to conflict of interest. "I'll take care of her, and Dad and I will go through all this information again. I want to make sure we haven't missed anything. Keep me informed of anything else you find."

"I will. If my schedule changes this morning, I'll let you know. I'm stopping by Lenora's on the way out of town. Then I'm meeting Taylor at the shopping center. We questioned people yesterday, but there were some we missed and others who might have remembered something to help us. After that, when the Lone Star Tavern opens for lunch, I'll be there."

"Talk to Jan Thomas again at Baby and Things. She's the cashier who's there most days. When I showed her the photo of the female kidnapper, like Lynn Davis, she thought she looked familiar but couldn't tell me why or where she saw her before." She sighed. "I wish I could come with you."

"Do you think she's holding something back?"

She shook her head. "No, I don't think so, but she may have seen something that she didn't realize might be important to us."

Dallas rose. "I'm sorry about last night in the chapel. I don't question you or doubt you. You know that. I'd work with you anytime."

Before Rachel could say anything in response, he walked out of the den. She started to go after him but wasn't sure what she should say. She cared about him and was desperately trying not to have any more feelings for him.

After Justin broke her heart, she wasn't sure she could ever risk her heart again.

# TWELVE

$\bullet$

At a little after ten, Dallas parked in front of the accounting office at the Chesterfield Shopping Center and called Rachel. "I wanted to let you know my mother is coming to the ranch to be there for Michelle."

"When?"

"She said something about bringing lunch for everyone, so probably in an hour or so. Is anyone up?"

"Yes. Mom's in the kitchen throwing away what's left of everything they ate last night. Deputy Jones told me he got samples of it all yesterday, and it's being tested. I checked on Michelle. She's still asleep. Dad is sitting here, trying to remember anything about last night. He's quite frustrated with himself," Rachel said in a low voice.

"I just arrived at the shopping center. I'll let you know if I find out anything that might help us. I called the detective on Lynn Davis's case. Nothing of interest was found at her apartment, but guess where they found the compact car? Behind the apartment building. It was impounded. The police are going over it."

"Great."

"Talk to you later." Dallas ended the call and climbed from the SUV.

They had discovered only yesterday that a Wi-Fi signal from the planted cameras in Baby and Things had been transmitted to a computer at the desk in an otherwise empty space behind the partition between the reception area and the rear part of the space at the accounting firm. He remembered looking in the window with Rachel that first day. They could only see what looked like a receptionist area. It had been empty at that time or possibly the person going through the video footage had been in the rear of the office. If only they had known, Katie and Chris Rand wouldn't have been taken, and they could have located where Brady was.

Dallas entered and called out, "Taylor."

He appeared from the back. "When will people learn that simply deleting a file doesn't get rid of it? I have IP addresses where some of the footage was sent."

"More than one place?"

"Yes. We'll have to check them all out."

"It's going to be a long day."

Taylor passed him a list with the places used over the past week—a library, a coffee shop, a restaurant and other public places. "I'll take the top half. You take the bottom half. The only thing we can do is show the female kidnapper's photo and see if anyone recognizes her."

Dallas's gaze latched onto the name of the Lone Star Tavern. That might be why Lynn Davis had recognized the photo, but why did they kill her? What else did she know? "Let's canvass the shopping center again, starting with Baby and Things. I'm still not convinced Steve Tucker isn't in the middle of this, although what you've found out so far doesn't send up a red flag. Also, Rachel reminded me that Jan Thomas, the cashier, thought she'd seen the woman somewhere other than the store."

"Like Lynn Davis. We need to be careful." Taylor was the last to leave the accountant's office. He locked it up before heading across the parking lot to Baby and Things.

"I think we should put a tail on her. Either she leads us to the woman or we have an officer there to protect her if someone comes after her. I don't want to question her in front of Steve Tucker. I'll talk to him while you question Jan Thomas. Caution her about mentioning the conversation to anyone else."

When Dallas stepped into the store, Carrie Zoeller and Betty Biden stared at him as he headed toward the rear where the owner's office was. He nodded at Jan and kept going while Taylor stayed behind to interview the woman again. As Dallas neared the closed door to Tucker's office, raised voices on the other side stopped him from knocking.

"The deal is off," a familiar deep, gruff voice said.

"I didn't do anything wrong," Tucker replied.

Dallas leaned his shoulder against the wall and waited for Tucker's visitor to leave.

"I don't know how to fix this. The press coverage hasn't been good for you."

Was that Richard Snapp, Tucker's lawyer? It sounded like him. Dallas thought of interrupting them, but he decided to see if he would hear anything that might help the case.

"This will put me back big-time. I've invested a lot of money in this."

"Me, too. Remember that," Snapp said to Tucker.

The door suddenly opened, and the lawyer strode out of the office, surprised at Dallas's appearance in the hallway. Snapp started to skirt around him, but Dallas stepped into his path. "I'm here to talk to Steve Tucker."

"Fine. I don't want to have anything to do with the kidnapping case." Snapp looked at his client. "I suggest you call a criminal lawyer, Steve."

"But I haven't done anything wrong." As Tucker watched his attorney leave, his eyes narrowed. "I guess it's a good thing he isn't handling my store expansion anymore." He shook his head. "It was his idea and things were going well—until now."

Dallas followed the man into his office and closed the door. "If we can close this case and clear your name, it might get better in time."

"That doesn't help me right now. As you could see when you came in, this store that's been doing well for years hasn't had a customer in the past day since the story hit the news. It doesn't help that reporters have been here this morning. I gave them a statement, but a few are still lingering, probably because of you com-

ing forward. "In less than a week, I'm ruined." his chair, his shoulders

"Now that we know the video feed was going to the accounting office across the lot, I'd like to know if you ever saw anyone going into or out of that place."

"I wish I could point you to the person who did this to me, but—" The shop owner stared into space for a moment. "Actually, I did one night when I stayed longer than usual. I was at the front of the store checking inventory when a woman came out. But it was dusk and her face was turned away from me. All I could see was long dark hair and big sunglasses. I thought that was weird since the sun had set. I usually go in and out by the back door, so that was the only time I can remember anyone at the accounting place, but it hasn't been here that long and it isn't tax season."

"Do you have any idea when you first remember seeing the digital clock on the back counter or the picture frame?"

Tucker hung his head. "Believe me, I would tell you if I remembered. I've been so busy with the details of the new stores in Houston and San Antonio that I haven't paid that much attention to the day-to-day activities here. Betty Biden and Jan Thomas might know."

Dallas put his hand on the knob to leave, glanced back and felt sorry for the man. Was he another victim of this kidnapping ring? He left the office and returned to the main store floor. Taylor was still talking to Betty at the front. Dallas decided to go ahead and interview Jan. They still had a lot of places to visit.

"Sheriff Young wanted me to talk to you again. She said you thought you had seen this woman before." Dallas showed her the two illustrations of the female kidnapper. _____ but sometimes wears a blond wig. Dark-brown hair where you might have seen her?"

"I've been trying. If I remember, I'll let you or Sheriff Young know. Please tell her I'm so sorry to hear about her daughter. I've been praying for them."

"I'll tell her."

He was turning to leave when Jan said, "Wait. I think I remember, but it was just a glimpse of her curly blond hair and sunglasses. It might not even be the same woman. She drove into this shopping center and pulled in behind the stores on the other side. I was leaving for lunch."

"When?"

"This Monday."

Before the kidnapping of Brady. "Thanks, Jan." Dallas joined Taylor as he wrapped up his conversation with Betty. "Anything from her?"

"No."

"Let's canvass the rest of the shops, then I need to go to the Lone Star Tavern."

"And I'll keep following the money trail."

Dallas left Baby and Things. Would that be enough and in time to save Katie? To get Brady before he disappeared, possibly in another country? He was running out of clues to investigate. *Lord, please help us. How do I face Rachel without one shred of information to pursue?*

Rachel stared at the papers strewn all over the games table in the den. She'd gone through them a second time and nothing. What was she missing? She stared at the map of Texas showing where the kidnappings they thought were connected took place. First in El Paso, then a couple of months later another cluster in north Dallas and finally, only a month later, in the San Antonio area, her attention riveted on the pins indicating Safe Haven Ranch and Dallas's sister's house. The only two kidnappings close to each other. The others were spread out, especially in El Paso.

A hand clamped her shoulder and kneaded the tight muscles. "Take a break, honey." Her dad took the seat next to her.

"I can't. I can rest when Katie comes home."

"But after a while it all becomes jumbled. Every-thing stops making sense. Believe me, honey, I've been there."

"Did you solve the case?"

"Yes, when your mother dragged me home. I'd been up for sixty hours straight. I took a good nap and then went back to the station with a clearer head. By the next day we had the murderer in custody. I have some good news. I just got a call that Rob is alert. He's still in critical condition but doing better."

She needed to let Dallas know about Rob. He'd want to talk to him. She couldn't see Rob doing that to the family, but she agreed he needed to be ruled out. "Dad, I think there's more to this than just the nine kidnap-pings we've seen. What if the ring is using several means to acquire babies and then sell them?"

"Like taking newborns, especially from women who don't want them but will take the money for their baby?"

"Or kidnapping young pregnant girls, then tak-ing their baby, then either paying them off or kill-ing them."

"I agree. We might only be looking at part of this baby-kidnapping ring. Sadly, it's going on worldwide."

Through the tears in her eyes, she stared again at the map. "Unless we find Katie, she isn't coming home, even if I do everything they say. Killing her means they would lose money. I'm putting on my uniform and going to town. First, I'm paying Rob a visit, and then I'll be at the station. Dallas and I think there's a mole, feeding the kidnapping ring information about the investigation."

His eyes grew wide. "The house was bugged. They could have found out that way."

"Yes, but it wouldn't have been easy to do unless someone was on the payroll."

"Are y'all considering Rob?"

She nodded slowly.

"Do what you need to do. I wish I could come, but I have to be here for your mom and Michelle."

"Is Michelle up? I haven't seen her since I came in here."

"Yes. She ate some breakfast and then went back upstairs."

"Did she say anything?"

"No. And I'm worried about her."

"I'll talk to her before I leave." She leaned close and gave her father a hug, then rose and left the den.

Ten minutes later, Rachel walked from her room, passing the open door of Katie's. She went inside and hovered over the empty baby bed with her daughter's favorite stuffed animal and blanket. She picked up the lion and rubbed its soft fur against her cheek, Katie's baby scent wafting to her nose.

"I'll find you, Katie. I promise." *Lord, Dallas said You can do anything. Please bring my daughter home safely to me. Please!*

As much as she wished she could stand here holding Katie's things, she needed to do her job. She put the items back in Katie's baby crib and turned to leave.

Michelle stood in the doorway, her eyes red, her cheeks wet with tears. "I couldn't stop them this time, either."

Rachel quickly closed the space between them, clasped Michelle's upper arms and pulled the teen close. "It's not your fault. You would have ended up hurt again." Or worse.

"I saw her come in and tried to grab Katie, but I fell. The room was spinning so much. I wanted to get up, but I couldn't." Michelle leaned back and looked Rachel in the eye. "I don't remember anything after that."

"Was it the same woman who took Brady?" Rachel asked.

"I don't know. All I remember is blond hair." Tears returned to the teen's eyes. "I couldn't protect Brady or Katie."

Rachel knew exactly how Michelle felt. She'd been saying the same thing since Katie was taken. If she hadn't been the sheriff investigating this case, her daughter would be safe. "We are not at fault, Michelle. It's the people who took them." She framed the teen's face and looked straight into her glistening eyes, her own tears barely held back. "Not us. We have to stop blaming ourselves." She remembered what Dallas had done with Michelle the other night that seemed to calm her. Maybe it would work now. "I have a lead. I'm leaving to follow it. Will you pray with me for both Katie and Brady before I go?"

"Yes! Dad says sometimes that is all we can do. And I'll continue when you leave."

Michelle bowed her head. Rachel took the teen's hands and did the same. As Rachel sent up a prayer to find Katie, Brady and Chris, the words washed through her, bringing a calm she hadn't felt since this case began.

Dallas entered the Lone Star Tavern at the end of the lunch rush and took a table against the wall facing the front entrance. He made a slow survey of the place and the people in it.

"Can I help you?" a woman in her forties asked him.

He briefly scanned the menu and said, "A hamburger and sweet tea, please."

"Fries or onion rings?"

"Onion rings." When she started to leave, Dallas asked, "I'm on a tight schedule. Will it be long?"

"Nope. About fifteen minutes. I'll bring your tea right away."

When the waitress left, he counted the number of employees—six. He needed to talk to each one. When the woman came back with his drink, he asked, "My name's Dallas, and I'm a Texas Ranger. I'm here on official duty." He flashed her his badge.

Her forehead wrinkled. "What? Is this about Lynn Davis?"

"Yes." He took out the illustration of both versions of the female kidnapper. "Have you seen a woman like her in here?"

She glanced at the one with blond hair but quickly moved to the brown-haired woman. She tapped the second drawing. "I've seen her a couple of times. I even waited on her last Friday."

"Was she alone?"

"Not last Friday. She was with a man."

Dallas pulled out his cell phone and found the photo of Jamie Johnson, her kidnapping partner. "Is this the man?"

"No, the guy was older with dark brown hair."

"Could you describe the man to a forensics artist?"

"Maybe, but you might be able to find it on the surveillance footage the tavern has."

"You keep your footage for a week?"

"We keep it up to a month. There was a fight in here last year. One of the participants sued the tavern. The footage was used to prove the staff did nothing wrong."

Dallas stood. "Where's the manager?"

"He's in his office." The waitress pointed in the direction of a hallway.

"What time do you estimate the woman was here last Friday with the man?"

"Lunchtime, about twelve thirty."

"Thanks. Box up my food, and I'll take it with me. I'll be in the manager's office." Dallas made his way down the short hallway and knocked on the door.

Dallas stepped into the office, showed the man his credentials and quickly explained why he was there. "Time is of the essence."

"Sure. I'm Timothy White." Standing, he shook hands with Dallas. "I'll help in any way I can. I've seen the stories about the baby kidnappings. I'm a father and it sends terror through me to think anything ever happening to my little girl." The manager turned to his computer and tapped a few keys. "What time and day?"

Dallas told him as he took a seat in front of the guy's desk.

Mr. White turned the monitor so Dallas could see the footage as they went through it in double time.

"Stop," Dallas said when he thought he saw the woman in question.

The tavern manager slowed the footage to regular speed.

"That's the couple. Can you zoom in? I need to do a screen capture of them."

"I can do that. I can print it out and send it to your phone."

"Great." Dallas stared at the man. He knew him, but not the name of the woman. "Do you know either one of them?"

"No, I'm usually in my office during the lunch shift. We're more crowded at night and that's when I'm out front. But you can ask the staff if they know."

Dallas took the photo from Mr. White, thanked him and left. The man wasn't necessarily associated with the kidnapping ring. It could be a coincidence. Or not. He needed the woman's identity to figure out who was behind the abductions. As he returned to the main part of the tavern, hope rose in him for the first time in days.

Rachel nodded at Deputy Carson standing guard outside Rob's hospital room. When she entered, she found the nurse checking Rob's IV. When she was finished, she left them alone. Rachel drew in a deep, calming breath and approached a man she'd known for years. Surely, he wasn't the one who'd betrayed her family.

She moved to the right side of the bed, forcing a smile to her face. "How are you doing?"

Rob's pasty complexion whitened even more. "Feeling dazed. I'm not even sure what happened."

"Your doctor said you might have died if Dallas and I hadn't gotten to the house when we did."

His dull gray eyes widened. "I remember eating and drinking tea, but nothing after that."

Which was what her parents and Michelle had basically said, but Rob's gaze slid away from hers. He stared at the foot of the bed. "What time was dinner?"

He shrugged one shoulder. "The usual." His body language screamed that something was wrong. Rob fisted the white sheet in his hands.

"I don't know if anyone told you, but Katie was kidnapped last night."

His head dropped forward. "What?"

"That's what I was going to ask you about. We found you and Dad in the den and Mom and Michelle in the kitchen—everyone groggy or passed out."

"What do they remember?"

Rather than reveal too much, she decided to conduct this interview as though Rob knew something. "The sweet tea was spiked with roofies, but you were also given an opiate injection intended to kill you. Why you and not the others? Do you have any idea how the kidnappers got into the house? When y'all were at the barn, the alarm system was on. After returning from there, everyone sat down for dinner. The door beeps when it's opened. That would have alerted y'all that someone was entering the house."

He swung his gaze toward her.

She glared at him. "Do you have any theories on how and when the kidnappers got inside the house?"

His attention returned to the foot of the bed as he twisted the sheet in his hands.

"Why did you do it, Rob?" Rachel asked in a quiet voice. When he didn't respond, she continued. "You were part of our family. Why did you betray us? My daughter is gone. They told me they were going to kill her."

His head shot up. "Kill her? They promised me

she wouldn't be hurt, and later she would be returned to you."

Anger welled up from the pit of her stomach. "And you believed them?"

"I didn't have a choice."

"You always have a choice."

"They had evidence I killed a criminal I was bringing in a few years back."

"Did you?"

"It was an accident."

"Who?"

"Fuller Patterson," he murmured in a thick voice.

"He was selling drugs to kids."

"I know. I was trying to get him to confess. I went too far. I can't go to jail. I can't..."

"Who recruited you? If you help us find the babies, it'll go a lot easier for you. I'll stand up for you." She needed his help, but he needed hers, too.

"I want a lawyer."

"As you know, that's your right to have one." Her voice softened. "But in the meantime, the longer Katie is gone, the better the chance we'll never find her—that the kidnappers will follow through and kill her."

"I met with her once. She told me her name was Audrey, but I followed her and found out where she lived. She thought her threat would totally cow me. She was wrong."

"Where does she live?"

Rob gave Rachel an address in San Antonio.

"Do you know her name?"

"Yes. Marilyn Peters and she lives with her brother."

Rachel started for the door, paused before leaving and said, "Thank you," then hurried out into the hallway to call Dallas.

\* \* \*

Dallas drove to the front of the hospital. Rachel exited the building and hopped into his SUV. One look at Rachel and all he wanted to do was comfort her. She put on a brave face, but when he gazed into her eyes, the hurt, sadness and fear were evident in those green depths.

"All right?" Dallas pulled away from the entrance to head to Marilyn Peters's house.

"I will be when I get Katie back. I can't believe Rob was the inside man. I don't know how many times he had an opportunity to go through our notes on the case. He fooled us. You think you know someone, but you really don't. This is how I felt when Justin told me he wanted a divorce."

"I know how you feel. I went through the same thing with Patricia. Her betrayal made me question my judgment, but I'm finding out if I carry that baggage around with me, I'll never get over what she did. For Michelle's sake—and mine—I can't do that anymore. Everyone makes mistakes. We must be willing to forgive, not so much for the other person but for ourselves. Hate eats away at people, gets in the way of enjoying life."

"So you've forgiven your ex-wife?"

Dallas glanced at Rachel, her lips pressed firmly together. "I'm working on it. Michelle blaming herself made me realize I had to, at least for her sake. But now I realize also for my own well-being."

Rachel's mouth relaxed into a neutral expression. "Michelle and I prayed together this morning for the babies stolen. I'd forgotten how good it felt to give the problem to the Lord. It's too big for me to handle alone."

"We're not alone when we go through the worst of times." Dallas's cell phone rang, and he clicked on his Bluetooth in his ear. "Taylor, did you find Richard Snapp?"

"No. He never showed up at work today. He must have left Baby and Things and disappeared because he isn't at his house, either. The other team at his home can't find any indication of where he would have gone. The same here at his office. I hope Rachel's tip will help us. In the meantime, I'm going to dig into Snapp's holdings and see if there's a place he could have gone."

"I'll let you know what I find at Marilyn Peters's house. We're not too far away." When Dallas ended the call, he told Rachel everything Taylor said.

"That man has my daughter. When I find him, he'll regret ever taking her, or rather, ordering Katie's kidnapping."

"We'll get Katie back. It's been less than twenty-four hours. Taylor is digging into any piece of property that Snapp owns. SAPD will join us at Peters's place. They should be there by now, waiting at both ends of the street. When we arrive, they'll join us."

"Good. Hopefully she's trapped but doesn't know it."

"We took extra precautions with her and Snapp as well. No one at his home or office was allowed to call out to warn him."

"She lives with her brother. He might be there, too. I don't know if the brother is involved or not. Rob didn't know."

"The brother could be the third guy we've been looking at. The one who killed the male kidnapper."

"How about anyone going out the back of her house?"

"Taken care of. Two police officers are posted behind her place."

"You've thought of everything."

"I'm only part of a team. The stuff Taylor has unearthed concerning Snapp indicates the man has the resources to get out of the country if we don't surprise him. He has a lot of contacts inside and outside of the US."

"Which could mean the babies aren't necessarily for people in the United States." Rachel folded her arms over her chest as though trying to warm herself. "You'd think after being in law enforcement for over eleven years, I'd get used to how low a human being can go."

"I've wondered that, too." Dallas turned onto a short street with nice homes with well-tended lawns. "We're going in fast. We can't let her contact Snapp. The two SAPD officers will go in the back at the same time. We'll quickly sweep through the house." He parked two houses away.

The unmarked SAPD vehicle pulled up right behind his SUV while another down the street took up a position several places away on the other side of Marilyn Peters's home. He reached into the backseat to gather weapons they might need. Rachel and he had suited up with their Kevlar bulletproof vests before they met at the hospital.

As he exited his car, he sent up a prayer for the safety of the team going in. One SAPD sergeant stayed behind to coordinate the groups. When Dallas reached the front porch, the police with the battering ram got into position. He put up three fingers and silently counted down, then the officers slammed their apparatus against the wooden door. It gave way on the second strike, and Dallas led the charge into the house, the sound coming from the back indicating the two breaching the rear were successful, too.

Marilyn Peters paused for a second halfway up the stairs, glancing over her shoulder at them. As she swirled around and continued up the steps, Rachel flew past Dallas, ascending only a few feet behind the female kidnapper. Dallas followed. At the top, Rachel lunged forward and pinned the woman to the floor. Rachel read Peters her rights as she pulled the kidnapper's arms behind her back and handcuffed her.

"Where's your brother?" Rachel asked.

The suspect shrugged.

Dallas moved in and helped Peters to stand. "You're under arrest on multiple accounts of kidnapping as well as murder and attempted murder."

"I didn't kill anyone."

Rachel got into her face. "So you admit kidnapping babies?"

"No!" Peters raised her chin and glared at Dallas and Rachel. "I want my lawyer."

"Who is that? Richard Snapp?"

"I don't know who you're talking about."

Dallas removed his cell phone and showed the woman the photo of her and Snapp together at Lone Star Tavern. "Then explain that. You have a choice. You can either go down for kidnapping, murder and attempted murder or you can make a deal for a lesser charge if you give us the whereabouts of Richard

Snapp." He gripped the female's arm and guided her down the stairs.

He sat her in the living room while the rest of the police went through her house. "If you were smart, you would waive your rights and tell us where Snapp is. He's not at his office or home. We're digging into every aspect of his life, and if we find where he is, you'll be charged with no deal for crimes that will put you in jail for the rest of your life."

"You don't have anything except a picture of me with Richard. He asked me out on a lunch date. I don't know him other than that time we were at Lone Star Tavern."

Rachel stepped forward. "His daughter identified you as the female kidnapper and Rob Woodward said you were involved with kidnapping my baby last night as well as trying to kill him."

The color drained from Peters's face.

Dallas stood next to Rachel and said, "Ah, you didn't know that Rob was alive and telling us about you recruiting him to help you. Time is running out for you. We'll find Snapp with or without your help. The deal is only on the table if you tell us where he and Katie are now."

"All I know is where Katie was last night. Richard could be long gone by now."

"Where?" Rachel's voice quavered.

Finally, Peters started to talk. Dallas wrote down the location of the ranch south of San Antonio that she mentioned and then turned her over to the SAPD sergeant. He and Rachel left the house and jogged to his SUV. As he pulled away from the curb, he placed a call to Taylor to coordinate the raid on the place, praying Katie, Brady and Chris were still there.

# THIRTEEN

Near dusk, Rachel looked through the binoculars at the layout of Snapp's ranch from a rise to the north of the main house. The San Antonio police had gotten more information from Marilyn about this place. She noted the building behind the barn that, according to the female kidnapper, was where young women were being held until they gave birth to their babies. Some of the ladies disappeared, and Marilyn didn't know what happened to them, and others had been at the ranch for a few years, becoming pregnant several times so far. Rachel didn't know if Marilyn was telling the truth about what exactly she knew. The very thought that women were held captive for breeding purposes chilled Rachel to the bone.

"If our intel is right, Katie and possibly Brady and Chris are still in the main house." Dallas set his binoculars down. "We'll be hitting there and the building behind the barn as soon as it's dark."

"The timing will have to be precise and quick, like at Marilyn's place, or Richard Snapp could harm the women and babies."

"We have to assume everyone at the ranch knows

what's going on. You can't have an operation like this for several years and keep it totally hidden from the cowhands and other employees working here." Dallas gestured toward two men mounting their horses near the barn then riding out toward a pasture to the west where cattle grazed.

"Most likely those guys aren't just cowhands but guards, too." Rachel donned her bulletproof vest, still remembering what Marilyn had said to her interrogators at the police station about why they risked taking Katie, Brady and Chris from their homes. Rich, important clients had certain criteria for the babies they wanted and paid handsomely for a child who fit those conditions.

"Ah, I see more pairs of cowhands are leaving and heading east and south."

Rachel watched the men ride off, then swung her attention back to the main barn. "Make that four groups of guards. This last one is coming our way."

"We'll take them down before moving toward the house."

Rachel glanced west. The sun was sinking below the horizon. Not too much longer. She desperately wanted to hold her daughter in her arms again. The waiting for darkness to fall caused her to pace among the trees as time slowly moved toward that goal.

Dallas stepped into her path. "Okay?"

"Yes. When we hit the house, my destination is the second floor, the bedroom at the end of the hall on the right side of the place. That's where the babies are kept until handed over to the couples who bought them." She would lead a small assault team upstairs, clear that level and secure the children while Dallas would search for Richard Snapp and make sure the first floor was safe.

"We need to check our equipment one last time before we move out."

She nodded, knowing the drill. This wasn't the first time she'd participated in a raid. She knew the dangers she faced as Dallas did, too. The main floor would be where most of the guards would be located. "Promise me you'll take care of yourself. Marilyn said there were at least six, if not more, guards in the house. They're familiar with the layout. We only have a rough sketch of the floor plan from Marilyn. What if she's leading us into a trap?"

He took her hands and held them up between them. "Then we'll just have to pray harder." Dallas bowed his head. "Lord, protect us and help us get the babies back, free the women and put an end to this evil. In the name of Jesus Christ."

"Amen." She wanted to feel that earlier peace she'd felt after praying with Michelle, but so many things could go wrong. She wanted Katie and the other babies back and Dallas unharmed. *Are You there, God? Do You hear us?*

"Let's go," Dallas said to the law enforcement officers from various agencies. "Taylor, you and your detail take out the two guards who rode out this way, then head to the building behind the barn."

Taylor nodded. "I'll keep you informed of our progress."

As his detail moved out to deal with the two guards, Dallas double-checked he had what he needed, put on his night-vision goggles and signaled the others to fan out and head for the main house. They used the cover available to keep their approach a secret. If he'd had any doubt this wasn't the right place, he didn't now. The guards patrolling the grounds right now wore night-vision goggles and were armed as though they were going into battle. Not your typical cowhands.

Near the house, three of his team, made up of local law enforcement officers and Texas Rangers, parted to cover the back entrance. The other eight would go in through the front with Rachel's group of four going upstairs. There was a lot at stake here. Usually when he participated in a raid, he wasn't personally involved, as he was in this case. Not just because of Brady, but he felt a connection with Rachel and her daughter. This had to work.

When they burst into the house, Dallas shouted, "Police." He heard the same from the three coming in the back entrance. His men fanned out while Rachel, gun in hand, started up the stairs. His team was to sweep through the left side of the house while the other in the kitchen would take the right side and clear it. One would be left in the entrance hall, guarding the front door.

Checking every place a person could hide, Dallas and his men cleared the library and crept onward, leaving behind one officer to guard their backs. As he entered a large sprawling room, a shot struck the door-frame near Dallas's head, and he pulled back. Then another rapidly sounded, coming from down the hallway they hadn't checked yet. The bullet hit him in the chest.

With three other officers, Rachel ascended the staircase. When she reached the second floor, she went first, glancing around the corner to view the hallway to the right then left. She signaled to the next two to go right while she and her partner went the other way. Three closed doors lined her end of the corridor. She opened the first one—a bedroom with a large poster bed in the center. While the deputy covered her back, she snuck forward, inspecting any place where a person could hide.

With each step she took, her heart pounded against her chest. When she reached the objective, she stood to the side and quickly opened the door. Using the wall as protection, she peered into the walk-in closet. Empty. Not even clothes were hanging up in it. As she backed away and started for the hallway, two gunshots reverberated through the air, the sounds coming from below.

"Texas Ranger Sanders is down," came through her earpiece.

She stiffened, her heart sinking into her stomach. Her first impulse was to race down the stairs and help Dallas. But there were six other men downstairs, much nearer than her. She had to find the babies.

After checking the bedroom across the hall, she tiptoed toward the last one, not wanting to give anyone a clue where she was. But when she stepped on a wooden plank that creaked, the loud noise announced her approach. Changing tactics, she inched toward the nearest door and pushed it open, ducking away from the entrance. When she eased forward, she swung into the room with her gun held in both hands out in front of her.

A nursery—with five baby beds, a changing table and a large dresser.

The sight churned her stomach because from her

vantage point she could see each crib was empty. She quickly moved through the area because there was no place to hide, except behind the two closed doors. After examining the closet with stacks of disposable diapers of various sizes, she headed for what must be a bathroom.

Another shot blasted from below. Then two more.

She glanced toward her partner, on guard at the exit. All she could think about was Dallas lying on the floor, possibly dead—and maybe others were, too.

"We're under attack, pinned down in the middle room downstairs," she heard over her earpiece.

She needed to finish and get down there. She quickly thrust the last door open and scanned the bathroom. With her back against the wall, she sidled toward a hidden nook where the toilet probably was. A vision in the mirror sent terror racing through her. Richard Snapp stood there, pointing a gun at her.

The force of the bullet that hit Dallas's vest threw him back against the wall in the hallway. He slid down to the floor, pain spreading outward as though a superhuman fist had plowed into his chest. With his hand still holding his gun, he lifted his arm and aimed toward the entrance as a man charged out of the room.

"Drop your gun," Dallas said as one of his partners closed in to help him.

The shooter came to a halt, glancing at Dallas holding his gun on him, then at the deputy with his weapon out and pointing at the man. He lowered his Glock, and Dallas's partner rushed in and took it from his limp hand.

A blast of gunfire, coming from the first floor on the other side, resounded through the house.

Dallas struggled to his feet, touching the place where the bullet lodged in his vest. "Let's get inside the room." He noticed the other deputy with him had ducked into the library they had cleared.

His partner took his handcuffs and secured the assailant with his hands behind his back. Then they moved into the sprawling long room with Dallas covering their backs. Inside, he hurried through it, making sure there were no more guards there, then took their prisoner and handcuffed him to a sturdy post. Dallas and his partner needed to be free to finish their sweep of the left side of the first floor while his teammate was keeping anyone coming down the hall from the front of the house.

He peered into the corridor. At least one person with a gun was in the last room on this side. He needed to make a move.

"We've neutralized three guards in the dining room. No sign of Richard Snapp," the sheriff from this county said. "All clear on this side."

Dallas inched out into the hallway but dodged back into the room when a man poked his head out and fired, striking the wall on the other side of Dallas. "We're under attack, pinned down in the middle room."

"We're on the way, coming from the back hall."

Again, a spate of gunfire resonated through the house, but this time from upstairs. Rachel!

Without hesitation, Rachel dropped to the floor and swiveled at the same time Snapp fired his weapon.

She lifted her gun and shot him in the leg. She scrambled forward while Richard Snapp went down. As she yanked his weapon from his hand and tucked it into her belt against her spine, she glimpsed Katie hidden between the wall and toilet, her daughter curled into a ball and covering her eyes.

A slight movement sent a wave of relief through Rachel as she said, "Mama is here for you, Katie."

Katie lifted her head. Her eyes grew wide, but she didn't move.

"Sweet pea, you're safe now. I'm not going to let anything happen to you." Rachel's attention shifted back and forth between her daughter and the lawyer groaning and trying to stop the flow of blood with his hands. "Come here."

Katie looked at the man between them.

"He won't hurt you anymore." She kept her eye on Richard Snapp while extending her hand toward Katie. Rachel felt her daughter's soft, trembling touch as she latched on to Rachel.

She wound her arm around Katie and lifted her up and over the lawyer while never taking her attention off the man behind the baby smuggling ring. After placing her daughter on the floor behind her, Rachel grabbed a towel and held it against the man's leg. She wanted him to live and go to jail for all he'd done.

"Rachel?"

Dallas is alive! "I'm in the bathroom. I found Richard Snapp. He had Katie. He's been shot."

When Dallas came into the room, Rachel glanced over her shoulder. He swung Katie up into his arms and moved closer. "The house is cleared. The last guard in the den has been neutralized. Only a pregnant teenage girl was found up here besides Snapp and Katie. One of the deputies is taking her in for questioning."

"How about Taylor's team?"

"The house behind the barn is secured." Dallas glared at the lawyer. "A lot of women are talking about what's been going on here at this ranch."

"I haven't done anything wrong," Snapp claimed. "I'm offering a service and helping these women. I'm financially taking care of them until they give birth, then brokering private adoptions for their babies. They have all signed papers to that effect."

"You can't explain away Katie being in your possession. Where are my nephew, Brady, and Chris Rand?"

Richard Snapp thinned his lips and looked away.

"If you don't cooperate with us, I'm sure someone in your organization will, and there's a paper trail we can follow, too. Where you go and how long you spend in prison is at stake right now."

Rachel stood and took Katie from Dallas. The feel of her daughter in her arms once again overwhelmed her. Before she cried in front of Snapp, she said, "I'll let Sheriff Baker know we need a paramedic up here. I'll also send a deputy. I need to get Katie away right now."

"Agreed. You should take her back to your family ranch. I'll take care of the cleanup here."

"Thanks, Dallas."

The adrenaline from the raid had begun to fade. Rachel moved to the exit with Katie resting her head against Rachel's shoulder. *Thank You, Lord. Those words don't even adequately describe how I feel. Please forgive me for turning my back on You.*

* * *

Later that night, Dallas climbed the stairs at the Safe Haven Ranch's main house. Exhausted, but at peace, he walked down the hallway and rapped against Michelle's bedroom door. He'd seen the light on and knew she was still up, even though it was after midnight.

Michelle opened the door and threw her arms around his neck. "Rachel told me that Brady was found with a couple, and you were taking him home to Aunt Lenora's. Is he okay?"

Tears welled up into Michelle's eyes. "And Katie is okay. Thanks for finding them, Daddy." She pressed her cheek against his chest. "I can't wait to see Brady tomorrow."

"Lenora hoped you would come over to her place as soon as possible in the morning. I'll take you." Dallas cleared his throat. He could have died tonight without telling Michelle how he felt. "Princess, we need to talk. These past few days have been so hectic, but I want you to know how much I love you. None of what happened is your fault, especially your mom leaving us. You're precious to me, and I'm honored to be your dad. Don't ever forget that."

Her eyes shiny, Michelle stood on tiptoes and kissed his cheek. "I love you, Dad."

He cupped her face. "It's your mother's loss for not being in your life. And I want you to always feel you can come to me about anything. We're a team, you and me."

"Thanks." Michelle smiled. "Now I can go to sleep. If you want to know where Rachel is, she's in Katie's room."

As Dallas covered the distance to where Rachel

was, his heart beat faster with each step he took. All he'd wanted to do was see her and make sure she was all right. The door was ajar, and he eased it open farther. Sitting in a rocking lounge chair, Rachel held her sleeping daughter against her.

Rachel's eyes locked with his, and he felt as though he were an eagle flying high up in the sky with a bright future spread out before him. He smiled as he closed the space between them. He'd kept her informed about what happened after she left to bring Katie home. All the people involved were arrested. Richard Snapp and any other injured people were taken to a hospital in San Antonio. In the weeks to come, he and Taylor would spend a lot of time shutting down all aspects of the baby smuggling ring across the state of Texas, but for the time being he intended to set his life right and get some well-deserved sleep.

He helped Rachel to her feet, and then she took Katie to her baby bed and laid her down. He came up beside her. "Michelle said she was okay."

"I think she will be. I'll do everything I can to wipe this incident from her mind." She turned toward him, the soft glow from the night-light nearby emphasizing why he was drawn to Rachel; she was beautiful on the outside and the inside.

He cradled her face between his palms. "It seems that I never thought I would fall in love again, but I am. I know that we haven't known each other long, but what I've seen in these past days makes it clear the type of person you are. Caring, loving and dedicated to her family and the people of the county she serves. That is so appealing to me."

"That's how I feel, too. Our partnership went beyond solving the case. When you face what we did together, you see a person in some of the worst situations. Your integrity and compassion are what I want. I never had that with Justin. I love you, Dallas, and hope we can see where this goes."

Before she said anything else, Dallas kissed her, pouring all his emotions into it. When they parted, he said, "I'm warning you, Rachel Young, that I intend to marry you when you're ready."

Rachel smiled and wrapped her arms around him, then tugged his head toward her. "I can't wait."

# EPILOGUE

*Four months later*

Rachel, in a short white dress, stood next to her husband of less than an hour at their wedding reception at Cimarron Trail Christian Church. The past four months since the downfall of the baby kidnapping ring had been a whirlwind. At the beginning of November, the last person involved in the ring, the one who'd killed the male kidnapper and Lynn Davis, had been captured trying to cross the border at El Paso. Marilyn's brother had been connected with a Mexican cartel where some of the babies were sent.

Dallas slipped his arm around her and held her close.

Then he nodded his head in the direction of Marvin. "I can't believe you invited him to our wedding after all he tried to do to you."

"I'm turning the other cheek. I have a lot to be thankful for, and the least I could do is forgive him."

He chuckled. "That's one of many reasons why I married you. I have no doubt you'll win that guy over eventually."

Rachel's mother approached them with a wiggling Katie. "I can't contain her any longer." She passed her into Rachel's arms.

Since the kidnapping, her daughter had been extra clingy, but it was getting better each day and she loved having Dallas and Michelle around.

Katie hugged her, then leaned toward Dallas. "Dada."

Dallas's eyes widened as he scooped her up into his embrace. When he turned to Rachel, he had a big grin on his face.

"What can I say? I have a smart daughter."

"And I'm one lucky man." He leaned over and kissed Rachel.

\* \* \* \* \*

Dear Reader,

Thank you for picking up the fourth book in my Texas Rangers miniseries. It's been my joy to feature these amazing lawmen working on different types of cases, to watch them at work.

The worst nightmare for a parent is a child's kidnapping. In this book, I wanted to show the heartache and devastation when a child is abducted from various viewpoints—from the family directly affected, from friends and family members, and from the people who work to bring the child home safely.

Being a law enforcement officer isn't an easy job, but it's especially difficult when a case involves babies and children. I want to thank all police everywhere who work tirelessly to bring to justice those people who think they can take advantage of the helpless.

I love hearing from readers. You can contact me at margaretdaley@gmail.com. You can also learn more about my books at www.margaretdaley.com. Sign up for my newsletter and get all the details about my current and upcoming projects every month.

*Margaret Daley*